CRANNÓG MEDIA

CRANNÓG 34 autumn 2013

Editorial Board:

Sandra Bunting
Ger Burke
Jarlath Fahy
Tony O'Dwyer

ISSN 1649-4865
ISBN 978-1-907017-27-8

Cover image by Harriet Leander
Cover design by Sandra Bunting
Published by Wordsonthestreet for Crannóg Media
Printed in the UK

Crannóg acknowledges the assistance of:

Galway City Council   Galway Language Centre   The Galway Study Centre

CONTENTS

FICTION

POETRY

The Galway Study Centre

Since 1983, the Galway Study Centre has been dedicating itself to giving an excellent education service to post-primary school students in Galway.

info@galwaystudycentre.ie
Tel: 091-564254

www.galwaystudycentre.ie

SUBMISSIONS

Please note new submission times.

Crannóg is published three times a year in spring, summer and autumn.
Closing dates for submissions are: November 30, March 31 and July 31.
Submission Times: Month of November for spring issue. Month of March for summer issue. Month of July for autumn issue.
Since we accept simultaneous submissions, these new times mean your submission is tied up for less time. We will not read *submissions sent outside these times.*
POETRY: Send no more than three poems. Each poem should be under 50 lines.
PROSE: Send one story. Stories should be under 2,000 words.

We no longer accept postal submissions.

When emailing your submission we require three things:

1. *The text of your submission included both in body of email and as a Word attachment (this is to ensure correct layout. We may, however, change your layout to suit our publication).*
2. A brief bio *in the third person. Include this both in body and in attachment.*
3. A postal address *for contributor's copy in the event of publication.*

To learn more about Crannóg Magazine, or purchase copies of the current issue, log on to our website:

www.crannogmagazine.com

FICTION

CREEPING   PAT O'CONNOR

I think I saw youngsters in the garden this evening, sneaking near the gate. The whole place is covered in bushes and trees and that's the only place you can see anything. I can't see much anyway. But I saw them.

I'd been meaning to try for milk and bread. Usually I go in the early morning, when no one is around. But often it gets too late. The pavements get busy and I have to wait another day. This evening I have to try, cos I've nothing left for days now. Milk was delivered here before Gracie died, when all this was flowers and lawns and paths. Now branches rub the windows, leaves block the gutters. A few short years and the trees are in. It's like they lie in wait, watching for you to get weak. They send in feelers like those youngsters do, testing the boundaries. One day, you look up – they're all around you.

Gracie wouldn't recognise the neighborhood now. It used to be... not well off, but it was good here. Everyone knew everyone. Everyone was the same. Then, after Gracie – they built those apartments. Looking right down on us practically. They broke Gracie's memory with that one stroke. Then three houses where the O'Malleys used to live next door. I stayed inside, to let things settle. To let them stop changing things. And they did, eventually, when they couldn't build anything else. They sent me a letter – would I consider selling the house? Gracie's house. That was the last letter delivered here. I went straight down – *furious!* – to the post office. No more letters please. No, not one. Ok, a collection box, I'll get them when I want them.

The pavements have become full of people. I don't know any of them. Young impatient couples. Prams and buggies. Toddlers, children squealing. Gloomy youths hanging around, making comments and sniggering. I thanked God then for the bushes. I didn't have to see those louts sitting on Gracie's wall. I could hear them though. Out on the street - bellows and screeches. Especially in the evenings. On school holidays, it goes on day and night – it's like the jungle. I dread calm days now. I pray for rain – it keeps them indoors. Any moment they might put the windows in on top of me. I've only one room left, rot is closing in like the bushes. But I must have food – milk at least. I can't carry on. But I can't go out. If only I could get milk delivered.

They're in the garden right this minute. I hear them. Rustlings. The crack of a twig. Low voices, somewhere in there. It is too much.

Behind a paint-peeled door, I find Gracie's rake. It's the size and weight I need, because my left hand doesn't close. I grasp the rake, tremble as I push along the path. My neck is stiff. I can't see forward when I stoop under branches, can only see my slippers inching along. Near the gate, the voices are in the laurel – low, miserable voices. My heart may burst. I have to wait a few minutes, until the pulse is slower. I say to myself – this is it. The time has come. I raise the rake, ease myself into the laurel.

There is a space, a cave of branches, with a sheet of plastic like a tent. A boy and girl, maybe ten years old; he is squatting, she is kneeling on cardboard. They are arguing sadly, putting something in a bowl. The boy has his back to me. The girl's face is wet, or is it just the light? I grip the rake more tightly, inching closer. In the instant she sees me, I am thinking of a den I had once near a railway line. I almost falter. But it's dog-eat-dog, and you have to pee at the pole. The boy is too quick but I get the girl on the knee. There is a flurry – screaming – a bursting through bushes. How many others there are, I do not know. I turn to make my escape.

By the time I reach the house, the wheezing takes all my energy. I lie against the half-stuck door until I get my breath. I judder the door in, try to close it. But it is swollen, sagged. It does not close anymore, so the chain is my lock. Leaves have gathered in the hall, ivy is snaking its way in. At least the chain still makes it. Thank God for the chain.

In the room, rubbish is piled against the walls. The only place you can still see the carpet is in front of the armchair. That smell of old milk cartons, the drone of the half-buried fridge, the crusted, dirt-shiny arms of my chair; these are my comforts. A brown stain has been spreading across the ceiling. It was halfway when I noticed it a long time ago, and a small piece of the bulge has fallen. I have a radio too, but I cannot play it: it fills me with the worries of other people. Also, I cannot hear sounds if the radio is on, and I need to know if they're coming. But the rake: I have dropped the rake. What betook me to use it? There could be reprisals, I see now. So I sit, cowled in my blankets, with the breadknife ready. Nothing comes. Is that a mercy or not? I no longer have strength. I want to get it over with. I would like them to come.

Evening has deepened. Darkness falls. Out in the street, roars and shrieks echo against the walls, the blare of loud cars and motorbikes is angry, ever-changing. I can't know who might be in the garden. The windows are useless because of the bushes. I dread those windows. I've dreamed of sheets of wood, of corrugated iron, so that when they come they must at least come by the door. But corrugated iron is as impossible as anything else. So I wait, for the yellow twinkling shapes on the wall to become grey with dawn. Then I can go out, onto the pavement, at least for milk.

When the room is bright, I boil the kettle and get the teabag. There is plenty of colour in it still. Enough for two days maybe. But I know I must not wait till the last. Not like last time. This time even the sugar is gone. I've pulled apart the old packets I can find, of sugar and biscuits. I've shaken them, even licked some of them. Lack of food is like a siren muffled by my skin. Black tea keeps me going, but it doesn't sustain me. I take so long at the tea that when I get to the front door, the shriekings of children echo from the street. I have missed it again. I must wait until tomorrow.

A day comes. Everything seems very bright. When I stand up, things get even brighter. I wait a long time before I can risk moving. I need something. But the teabag would take too long, and I have not another day to lose. No sound of youngsters, so I release the door-chain and start along the path. Even under the bushes everything seems unusually bright. Yet I cannot distinguish twigs or leaves. Near the gate, I get fearful. What if they are waiting? What if their burly parents are here? I wish I had the rake. I push into the laurel, fearful, to get the rake.

How beautifully still everything is under the bushes. It is dry and peaceful – there is no movement, no noise. The plastic sheet is still there. The rake is there, at the side. Where the girl kneeled on the cardboard, there is a white tub, half-knocked, with some water, and a blue plastic bowl with brown stuff in it. When I move, bluebottles buzz from the brown stuff, and settle again with their darting runs. It is food. My stomach bubbles. The tongue sticks to my lips. This will be degrading, I know, but I am a long way from the shop and nothing is for certain. I will have to get on my knees. There is a box I can lean on, under the plastic sheet. In the box is newspaper, and something dark is on the newspaper. An animal. I pull the box out to see. It is a puppy, smooth and tan coloured, lying on its side. It has too much skin and it is very still. But there is movement at its eyes. White things, like crumbs of bread. Maggots. The eyes are gone. I nudge the body, and a ripple moves along its fur. Its paws curl minutely. It is not dead.

I look away, into the stillness of the bushes. I see there an image of myself lying, waiting for the flies to realise that I cannot even blink. Then, when my tongue cracks, the magpies and crows and rats would come. There is no pity under the bushes. I kneel for a long time.

Eventually the shouts of children begin, as every day. I only vaguely hear them, because I am thinking now that I must take up the rake and finish off this unfortunate creature. I lift the body from the box. Its tiny sagged movements, the twisting of the maggots, are excruciating to me. I lay it on the cardboard, and shuffle to where the bushes overhead will allow me one good swing with the rake. I raise it, bring it down as hard as I can. Raise it again, to be certain.

There is a snap of a twig. I freeze – it is the boy, creeping, almost in the clearing before he sees me and the rake and the shivering body of the pup. His face stretches. He flounders and blusters in the bushes and is gone.

Like a thump, it hits me what he must feel. That I killed his pup. That is what he will believe, in his head and in his heart, and he will make war against me. But in his soul he will know – I know he will know – that he has simply been too long away. Like I was, for that single weekend I went to a conference of steam trains in England. I was away four days. When I came back she was on her face in the hall. Her arms were perfectly at her sides. Everything was absolutely perfect, but she was cold.

The boy has dropped a plastic water bottle – it is still wobbling – and a box of something. That, I am sure, is food, and I think maybe, maybe... if I can just ... But it gets very bright under the laurel. Too bright. I know in my heart that it is too bright altogether.

Something is moving. The boy. He is in the bush again, in a glistening plastic coat. Dripping. There is the smell of earth and wet leaves. He bends low, like he is peeping into a burrow, to see into my eyes. Rain drips from his hood. His black wellingtons creep toward me. I cannot move. I am a skin filled with broken glass. The boy edges forward, bends again wide-eyed to see. The handle of the rake has become darkly wet. His soft pink fingers curl around it, and he lifts Gracie's rake from my hand. I think: a bang on the head would be like a comforting quilt. If only he has the strength.

ANONYMOUS LIFE   FIONA WHYTE

There is a small fire in the corner of the room. Winter is in my fingers and as they grip the reed, the pain ekes out into the ink, blotting the parchment with its black scratches.

Cuthbert is dying. I must record these last moments, his final message. The brothers pray for one more miracle, that his dying breath will give dumb Aidan voice or cure Engelbert of his stomach sickness.

We lost Lawrence on the crossing to the island. A sudden wind and frantic movement. No one heard him fall into the black water. We told Cuthbert, hoping he might tell us where to search and maybe he did but his voice is weak, dying before him. Sometimes I put my ear to his cracked lips and scratch his words onto the goat skin but I cannot see their meaning.

We fear his death. Although he has cured illnesses and halted plague and even restored the widow Anna's son to life when all doctors had despaired, we dread these things will end with him; they will not matter. It is as if God himself is dying.

I tremble before this great task ahead of me. Prior Herefrith has been stern in his admonition that I must write the first story of our noble Cuthbert. It must contain the full and true account of his blessed life, lest later versions become corrupted by false rumour or misunderstandings. There are many witnesses. They have brought all their stories. I must write the truth, just as they tell it.

Herefrith trusts me. That is why I have been chosen, though Brother Wilfrid is known for his powerful words, and these days most other scribes in the monastery have a better hand than I. My quill will not make the page sing or cause men to weep, but, if God wills it, I will put down in plain words the deeds of Cuthbert.

This is what is needed for now says Herefrith, a record of Cuthbert's deeds as recounted by the witnesses. How he put out a fire set by the devil, exorcised the wife of a sherif and cured the Abbess

Aelfflaed. Later, one like Brother Wilfrid will take these simple lines and through the power of the Spirit breathe fire into them, turn them to verse perhaps with strong words which will exhalt great Cuthbert and cause his name to live forever. And this is how it should be, for I cannot see how my feeble words can be a light to any man.

I consider too the vanity of creating my own words instead of transcribing His. But Herefrith says that to preserve forever the greatness of Cuthbert's deeds is to glorify the name of our Holy Lord. These are a simple people here, suspicious of any who come from beyond the village boundary. They sniff at stories of a man from a place called Galilee, a name that does not sit well on the English tongue, does not carry the heaviness of Monkwearmouth or Coldingham. Cuthbert is one of theirs. They will hear of his marvels and come to the Risen Lord through him. But they will come only if God unknots my fingers and breathes words into them.

When Cuthbert travelled out here to the Farne, he found the island a desolate place. Spirits of the devil's hosts lived here and tried to drive him out. He had little food or water and no shelter. But God sent angels who gave him strength to lift stones which should have taken ten men to bear. Within one night he had built this simple dwelling and the oratory beyond. In the morning, thirsty from his night's labours, he went in search of water and finding none, blessed the barren ground, dug a hole and a spring of water gushed forth. It still provides us with the only fresh water to be found on the island.

He is more agitated now. Herefrith and I draw closer to him and Herefrith soothes him with a blessing. Perhaps his old tormentors have returned to taunt him in his weakness but I am certain that even now he will withstand them.

I have known these demons too. They are relentless in their quest to drive us from the true path and they are everywhere. There were many in the monastery at Lindisfarne. They lived in the gardens where I first worked as a young monk. We were encouraged to recite the psalms silently as we sowed seeds and turned the soil. I would imitate the other brothers and move my lips to the words and try to see nothing but the patch of earth where I laboured; then I would sense the enemy at my back, drawing my tongue from the sweet words of the psalmist, filling me with thoughts of previous times and persons better forgotten.

Looking at the rows of cabbages, I saw not the soil of Lindisfarne but the gardens at Melrose where I was born. I could smell the dampness of the grass in the late evening and hear Theodore, my brother, calling me while he hid in the apple trees or behind the well. It seemed to me that he called me away from the monastery to come and find him again, and that the salty droplets on my cheeks were the tears he cried on the day the monks came to take me away.

God didn't want me said another demon. I was nothing to Him, just another child fostered out to be one of His many servants, an insignificant offering from a noble family. I had no gifts, could not tell a mint leaf from a nettle. I failed to see the light of the Gospels, my recitations of the Hours were empty sounds and my prayers, when I could form them, did not ascend to Him but tumbled to the ground, lifeless and cold.

I begged to be allowed to work indoors where I felt the walls of the hallowed monastery would afford me more protection. They sent me to the kitchens where Brother Ingwald guarded my every movement and if my fingers found rest for even a moment he filled them with more labour. My hands blistered with sores, my knees chafed and still the enemy sought me out.

They entered my cell between Compline and Matins, with words of torment, planting vines of doubt which grew and twisted their branches around my heart until my breath came only in short gasps and my limbs refused to obey my commands. Then the time came when I lay in my cot all day ensnared by the fiend, prayed no longer and spoke to none.

A heavy fog had descended upon me, through which God's light did not penetrate. I felt the weight of this fog as though it were a thousand boulders. It bore down upon me and pressed me hard to

15

the ground while all the time voices like the devil's spit told me that the One sent on earth as Saviour could not save me, that the only peace to be found was beneath the cold earth.

Cuthbert came to see me. He took my hands in his. He examined the sores. He heated water and bathed them, turning then to my knees and feet. He gave me to drink some warm wine and sat in my cell until dawn, praying without cease. The demons did not come that night.

In the morning he raised me from the cot and had me brought to the scriptorium. A sharpened reed was placed in my hand. On the desk was a sheet of fresh goat skin alongside a sheet of manuscript. One of the monks had copied in fair hand the first chapter of the Gospel of St. John. 'Write,' said Cuthbert, and again, 'Write.'

I feared to write these holy words. I feared greatly that the enemy would enter my hands and cause me to corrupt the page with vile blasphemies and false utterances. But I feared disobedience of my Holy Prior more and so I bade my fingers to dip the reed into the ink pot and made my first scratches. 'In the beginning was the Word.'

Many times I wrote these verses before my craftsmanship came to please Prior Cuthbert and to be accepted for binding in a manuscript, and although I have not received the gift of creating pictures to illumine the Holy Word, still I have created fair letters.

I wrote and wrote for many months and years until my hand assumed a twisted form. Marking God's words onto the parchment protected me from the demons and when they sometimes sought me out at night in my cell, I would make my way to the scriptorium and write until they retreated, unwilling were they to enter battle with Holy Scripture.

But since Cuthbert has gone to live in seclusion on the Farne I have been troubled by great pains in my hands. My fingers refuse to unbind themselves. Every incision on the parchment sends tremors from my fingertips to my neck and many times lately I have wished to be released from my duties in the scriptorium. I have grown weary from the strain of forcing words from the quill and feel a great longing to live all my hours in prayer and solitude as noble Cuthbert has shown us. It is not for all, he has said, and should the devil appear with his legions would I be able to battle him with spoken words only? Yet it would afford me some release from the torment in my hands and free me from the burden ahead.

He beckons me again. This time he speaks more clearly. 'Write,' he says. 'You will write.' I put my hands to his mouth and hold them there. I feel the lightness of his breath flow over my knuckles and fingers, warming them. Slowly I slip the reed into my knotted fist. The words come.

I begin.

TALL ARE THE PINES FAR AWAY RON D'ALENA

Clothed in flannel pyjamas, Clara was sitting at the kitchen counter when she heard a car come up the drive and into the carport alongside the house. Through the window above the sink she surveyed the scene. The light of day was fading. Grey clouds moved across the Spokane sky, concealing the far-away foothills crested with mature and hardy pines. In the carport, Mama slammed the car door and made her way around the rear of the station wagon. And as she hurried toward the front door she shivered and pulled her jacket tighter about her body.

The front door opened. Mama stepped into the living room from the front porch. A gusting wind blew past her, cold, oppressive. She closed the door, shed her jacket, hung it from one of the hooks on the wrought iron coat stand against the wall. Then she used her palms to smooth the wrinkles in the skirt of her blue and white waitress uniform. The backs of her arms jiggled with the motion. 'It's brass monkey cold out there, I'm telling you,' she said.

Pushing her tangled red hair from her face, Clara looked anxiously into the living room, past Mama. She squinted at the laundry piled upon a couch under the window overlooking the front yard and street, and she began rubbing her forefinger over a thumb calloused from twenty-seven years of working the metal wheel of a cigarette lighter. 'Before you even ask...' she said, 'no, I didn't fold the clothes.'

When Mama saw the pile she let her purse drop to the floor. She said, 'Listen, I'm glad to have my little rabbit living with me again, but when you moved back home you agreed to do the housekeeping.'

For a moment Clara recalled her move back home. Just a while ago she had lived downtown with Stutz, in a tenement house squeezed between the Conaco station and the red-brick building that was the Baptist church.

Mama said, 'Are you listening to me, goddamit?'

Clara stared at Mama's scolding lips, the dull lipstick. Only then did she notice the split lower lip. Leaping from the kitchen chair and moving quickly into the living room, Clara patted Mama's back and tried to get a closer look. She said, 'What the hell happened, Mama? Is this Boyer again? I thought you quit that son-of-a-bitch!'

Mama's cheeks reddened. She jerked away from her daughter and went into the kitchen. 'The hell with Boyer, this conversation isn't about Boyer,' she said. 'It's about you.'

'Me?'

Clara watched Mama get a bottle from the fridge and pour a glass of wine.

When Mama returned to the living room she said, 'What have you done for me lately? I mean name one thing you've done for me without me having to ask.'

'I do lots of stuff around here.'

'You can't even fold the clothes when asked.'

'Mama...'

'What do you do all day long, huh? I'd like to know. Tell me.'

'Okay, since you asked... I think! I sit around and tell myself that I'm not worthless and stupid and that the bad things that happened in the past aren't my fault.'

Mama sipped her wine, then became thin-lipped. 'Anyway,' she said, 'you were always a very lazy little rabbit.'

'Oh, for fuck's sake, Mama...'

Mama took up a book of matches and a pack of cigarettes from the coffee table next to the TV and lit a cigarette. Then she touched the cut on her lip and looked at her fingertip. 'From now on I want you to keep up with the chores,' she said flatly. 'And if you don't keep up you're out.' Then she went into the kitchen, got the bottle of wine and moved down the hallway to her room.

Clara worked her thumb against the metal wheel of her lighter. She lit a cigarette, then went over to the couch and began sorting the laundry. She put her clothes on one side of the pile, Mama's on the other side and towels and washcloths on the window sill above the couch. Living with Stutz, she thought, had been bullshit. She thought they could make something together. Instead he gutted her with whiskey and the back of his hand and his belt buckle.

Clara glanced up from the laundry. Through the window over the couch she saw Mr. Brinkman. He was on the other side of the street, standing beneath the Z-shaped fire escape hanging over the entrance to his shop. He was a tall, wiry man with a receding hairline. He stood there smoking, taking a break from his engraver's workbench. For quite some time now he'd been foolheaded over Mama. He was a decent guy, Clara thought, no hot number, but a decent guy. She was sure Mama would be receptive to him if Boyer weren't hanging around. Leaning across the couch, she banged on the window and waved to Mr. Brinkman, but he continued to smoke without acknowledging her. And as he stepped out of the wind to a spot alongside a window showcasing trophies, plaques and custom etched glassware, a tow truck pulled slowly up to the kerb in front of Clara's house.

Boyer got out of the truck, went to the edge of the driveway, stopped. His thick neck jutted up from his mechanic coveralls, leaving his skin exposed to the snapping wind. He started up the driveway, stumbling from side to side, staring at the ground as he walked. Clara wondered how he was able to operate his truck in this condition and she told herself that he would never make it to the top of the drive without going down. But he did make it to the top.

Clara hurried to the front door, stepped out onto the porch, shut the door behind her. The smell of oncoming snow was on the wind. She began to shiver. Her neck hurt with tension. Boyer looked at Mama's station wagon in the carport.

'I see she's home now,' he said.

'She's sleeping.'

'I swung by Alex's Café after she got off work. She looked tired.'

'You hit her.'

'She was tired and got a little out of hand. But things are fine now. She told me to stop by after my last call.'

Clara folded her arms below her breasts. 'She doesn't want to see you anymore, Boyer. She told me so when she got home.'

Boyer moved up close to her, leaned forward, wavered on unsteady feet. The reek of alcohol was strong and stale. 'I don't think so,' he said. 'She was a little out of hand but I forgave her and now things are fine. So how about moving out of my way and letting me in out of this cold.'

Clara became indignant. 'Fuck off, Boyer,' she said, 'Mama doesn't want to see you anymore.'

'Now don't go pissing me off, little girl,' he said. 'Just move on out of the way and let me in.'

'You ought to go away,' she said. 'You ought to go away now before I call the cops.'

'I'm telling you, you'll be sorry.'

'Please just go ...'

'You'll be sorry if you don't let me the hell in.'

Clara looked across the street at Mr. Brinkman. He stood at the entrance of his shop cupping a cigarette to his lips. He was looking down at the sidewalk and the wind took up the smoke coming from between his fingers and carried it past the window showcasing his engravings. She returned her attention to Boyer, looked at him closely. There was no decency in his face. It was difficult to believe Mama had any sociable feelings toward him at all.

Boyer staggered backwards and looked past Clara to the front door. 'Irene!' he called. 'Jesus Christ, Irene, let me in!'

Clara began rubbing her forefinger over her thumb callus. 'I'll scream,' she said, and she hollered into the wind to Mr. Brinkman. 'Hey Brinkman!' she yelled.

But Mr. Brinkman was busy lighting another cigarette and showed no notice to her.

Boyer bent down and picked up the end length of garden hose

which lay coiled in the mud next to the porch step. The threaded metal tip was muddy and a little bent.

'What are you going to do with that thing?' Clara asked.

'I'm going to beat your head with this if you don't let me in,' he said coldly. 'I'm going to beat your head, then I'm going to find your mother.'

There was a noise. Clara turned and Mama was standing there with wine-glazed eyes and tousled hair. And as they looked at each other Clara heard the metal tip of the hose clank against the concrete.

'Now you see,' said Boyer, 'your mother's here to make things right. Aren't you, Irene?' He pushed past Clara and stepped in close to Mama and hugged her with his thick arms and his cold breath went against her cheek.

Mama frowned. 'What the hell's going on out here?'

'Nothing, nothing,' Boyer said, and he led her into the living room and used his arm to clear the folded clothes from the couch onto the carpeted floor.

Mama looked confused. 'You got some nerve coming around here,' she said defiantly. But when Boyer told her to lie down she stretched out on the sagging pillows and let him put a wrinkled towel behind her head. Then she said, 'I forget what we was fighting about.' Her voice was hoarse, her tone fatigued.

Clara hurried into the living room. The pulse in her temples pounded as she yelled at Boyer. 'Mister,' she yelled, 'I want you out of here right now!'

Boyer lay down on the couch next to Mama, half his body hung over the edge and it looked to Clara as if he would roll off onto the floor like two hundred and fifty pounds of chopped wood.

'Clara,' Mama said, 'be a good little rabbit and get that bottle of wine from my bedroom and another glass from the kitchen.'

Just for a moment Clara saw everything as a stranger might see it – the threadbare couch, the age-yellowed kitchen linoleum, the dirty walls, Mama's faded looks and high-strung loneliness. Slowly she realised she was looking out the window and that her eyes were locked with those of Mr. Brinkman. Then the moment was over and Mr. Brinkman dropped his cigarette to the concrete and went into his shop and she was left looking at Mama's split lower lip.

'Mama,' Clara sighed, 'you're fucking up again. You can do better than this.'

Clara twisted her hair into a bun and went down the hallway to her room. She shut the door and sat down on the edge of her bed. A hush filled the house and rain began to pitter patter against the roof. Mama and Boyer came down the hallway and Boyer pounded on Clara's door a few times before going to Mama's bedroom. Mama stopped and spoke through the door.

'Don't worry, little rabbit,' she whispered. 'It's all been a horrible misunderstanding. Everything is fine now. Boyer is nothing like your father so don't you go worrying yourself over nothing.'

The hallway floor creaked as Mama went to her room. Clara heard the bedroom door shut, then she heard their laughter. The rain was now coming down hard. Gusting wind moved over the Monroe Street Dam, skimmed through the deteriorating neighbourhood, rattled her window. She used her lighter, got a cigarette going. She reclined against the oak headboard. The wood was cold through her pyjamas. Then she drew a breath from her cigarette and closed her eyes and held the smoke deep in her lungs until she felt hollow and a little dizzy before exhaling.

GODS   STEPHEN SHIELDS

Gods make their own importance. Patrick Kavanagh

- I smote him.
- You what?
- I smote him. Turned him to ash. His life flashed before his eyes in seconds.
- You never said you'd been married before.
- It wasn't a priority. I had this new life to begin.... A new country.... In a world that no longer understands.
- Understand! Understand what? That you've got a skeleton in your cupboard.
- The fickleness of Fate. That sometimes a girl has to do what a girl's got to do. Maybe one day she finds her equal. Till then, anything she fancies.
- Arrogant bullshit. Bitch. Are you going to tell me that no-one can hold you to account for what you've done? That I shouldn't get respect from you.
- You can change that oil yourself! Really, do you expect me to soil my pretty little hands? After I've spent hours doing my nails!
- Your nails. You want to talk about a manicure, and you've just admitted you killed your first husband.
- Who said he was my first? Remember, you're married to a legend.
- Legover, more likely! You'll probably tell me you slept with Zeus, the shipping magnate, next.
- Sleep! I'd have better things to do with my time, if a real idol crossed my path.... Sleep? That's what I do, when you come groping.
- I'll remind you, girl, that you were happy enough to hop into my bed when I met you.
- Yes, when I heard you had a business and a quick ticket out

of that country, where, nowadays, no-one understands a free spirit.

- You didn't impress me, but I needed someone for this whole thing to gel. Eye candy. That's all you were. To distract the customers with the laser accuracy of their own lechery, while they waited for their fish 'n' chips. And you had a healthy colour compared to the pasty faces who hang out around here.

- Eye candy for you more like. You couldn't hack it on your own, where the sun won't shine. You needed someone to lift you out of your dejection. Well, are you going to change that oil?

- Change that oil! Change that oil! You think you can tell me what to do! Who brought who here? Who's in charge? This is my chipper, you know! You're here for a purpose, not to rule the roost. I picked it. Found it here at the end of the alley, where all the night owls end up. After their hours of carousing, they all come to The House of Hades. And you're going to tell me to change the oil now! Just get to it!

- I'm not discussing it.

- Like you had nothing to discuss with that late husband of yours. Well, I'm no innocent to lie down and die, at your whim. I'm king of my castle. You don't play with me.

- King of the castle? It's only a grotty chipper at the end of the road. King of the deadbeats. King of the desperate. Even the dregs around here can't stomach what you serve. You're out every morning, trying to wipe the crust of their puke from your back alley doorway. Is this all you think I'm worth? Never mind that half of my year is spent without any sunlight in this last post for humanity.

- This is your last call to change that oil. Customers will be flocking in that door soon, and they want to see golden chips. That's what sets their mouths drooling. That's my profit.

- Your profit. Your oil. Change it yourself.
- Do I have to make you do it?
- Make me do it? I'm the one around here with experience of getting things done, my way. Mind!
- Yeah! The husband in flames trick. Try it on me. See how far you get.
- You can sluice that oil down the lavatories for all the chance you have of me lifting a finger here this evening.
- What about our agreement? You work hard here, the place prospers and you get to have a holiday at home every year. Forgotten our little agreement, have we?
- This place isn't all you cracked it up to be, is it? Cosmopolitan city, scenic river, concerts by all the big groups. Adopted home of Orfeo, the greatest!

  But you didn't say we'd be stuck out here in a drab suburb, some almighty flyover keeping us in the shade, day and night. Nothing to look at but the back end of lock-ups.

  Boom! boom! from the clubs all night. That's as close as we get to music.

  And as for visits home, when exactly did they happen?
- You've got to earn your rewards. Keep your end of the bargain. Stop this *the world doesn't show respect anymore* crap. Things change. Think how the scales of Fate teeter. Sometimes shit happens and you wait for the carousel to come around again.
- That damned shadow from the flyover is nothing like a cool lie down under the canopy at the Parthenon, is it? And, O for a view.
- Forget your daydreaming. There's a chipper to be run here. Just get the oil sorted.
- You and your stinking oils. All we've scorched and poured down the drains. No wonder we don't go to the river. You've probably turned it to sludge with your run-offs. In the old days, I would just have taken flight from such tedium. Left

a mark of my displeasure.

- These aren't the old days. Some days the sun doesn't shine, so get with the programme. The quicker you get to it, the quicker it's done. Then, there might be some hope of profits. Then, you can talk of the old days.

- You like it down here in the shadows, don't you? No-one to upset your boring little world. No-one to challenge you. No fear that life would jump up and give you a nip. God, you're like Cyclops in his cave. One of those eyes false, eh?

- Don't try me! Many a man has felt my smite. I've a whole world that you've never noticed. People respect me for it.

- I'm not bothered by your crazy world. My family controls its own corner of creation. Didn't you know that? That's how we reached our bargain. You met my mother. She did explain all that to you, didn't she? Or were you just too dense to understand her?

- There's a lot she didn't tell me, like about that late husband of yours. A fine family, alright. Daughter a killer, mother a conwoman.

- Careful what you say about my mother. I'm touchy about my family.

- Just change the oils. For all your talk, you're going nowhere. What choices have you got? Go back to where you're a wanted woman? I don't think so.

- What do they want me for? Who knows me? What exactly is there to find in my past? Only a pile of fine ash well worked into the soil of Mummy's vineyards.

- I could talk. I know enough about your past to go digging, expose your little secret. Maybe dig up some more.

- You're getting into deep waters. Not good for a little man who hasn't seen more water, in years, than he can piss from a senile bladder.

- Watch it, lady. Around here, I'm the one who barks loudest. Just check the title deeds. See whose name is on the bank account.

- Some bank account! There's nothing to it but a few greasy notes from that till over there. My family could rustle up enough small change at breakfast to show how puny your fortune is.
- Your family? A bunch of halfwit farmers scrounging in the sun to make a few olives ripen. Go; get the pressings of some of those olives, so we can make money here in the night-time, where the real profits are.
- You're heading into fiery territory.
- You've talked enough. Just change the oil.
- I don't think I shall.
- Just do it.
- No, I'm in no mood for a little Takeaway. Look at these nails. Perfect. I'm not damaging them for your slimy French fries.
- You could regret this.
- How? Brave enough to make me?
- It could be a long time before you see the light of day again.
- Take it easy. Your cholesterol could rise up your gullet and choke you.
- Cheeky, aren't we? So you think you can put the frighteners on me.
- That won't be necessary!
- What's that smell? Who's turned on the fryers? Jesus, they must be burning at four hundred degrees centigrade.
- At least. Just right for a roasting!
- It was you, you cow. You did this, so you wouldn't have to do the filters and change the oil.
- Not quite! I think it's just reached the right temperature ... O look, you've gone and slipped ... It's working perfectly. As always ... Just slide the rest of this foot in that way ... Better ring Mummy.

Hello Mummy. Yes, Caprice here.

Yes, Mummy. It's happened again.

Mummy, you know I don't like it when you use my real name.

But Mummy, he practically lit the torch himself.

What do you mean you can't afford another cover-up?

You agreed what with him to get me off the hook?.... Half our production mortgaged.... Sealed and notarized.... On your uppers!....

Can't you do something for your little girl, Mummy?... Is that your last word, absolutely?.... But it's so dark here, Mummy.

And the people are the same colour as Zombies.

THE CRANES   RHUAR DEAN

Rumour had it that they were building cranes over in East Street Market. Great big fuckers, the kind that scrape at the sky. I had to see it. I had to get there and climb up on one and maybe, just maybe, jump off – out into the sea of faces below.

The fever was in me. The rush and the swoon of a warm summer evening and all of the women seemed to be wearing short skirts. There were lorries everywhere, backing up into every space on the road to bring more rungs for the cranes. The world had an incessant beeping and robotic voices spouted warnings at each turn.

I ducked into the bookies to place a bet, remembering as I left that I wouldn't be around long enough to cash it in. *I bet I win,* I told myself. *I bet I fucking win.* The thought was distressing. I sat down for a while and considered my options. *I mean, I was going for the cranes. The big fuckers. The kind that scrape the sky. And there was no way, absolutely no way, I would survive the fall.* It made my brain freeze and my chest tight. I jumped around for a minute in frustration, mincing between a small crowd of Muslim women and tipping my hat to them like a jolly jester. They didn't laugh. They barely even looked. *What was I, invisible? Was I not even there?*

'Hey!' I shouted at an old man. 'Hey!' I waved my hands in his face. He saw me alright. 'Piss off,' he said with a wheeze and an arthritic flick of his wrist. I kissed him for seeing and he punched me clean on the nose.

Someone else grunted at me and pushed me along the street a way, holding me by the arm with a tight grip. 'Have you seen the cranes?' I asked. 'The big fuckers, the ones that scrape the sky?'

'Yes I've seen them,' he said. 'I've seen them and they're big and yellow and they go up forever. There's a springboard at the top and people like you just floating off them and away into the clouds.' He pulled me close to him. 'The queue goes off round the corner – you'll be there for days waiting if you even find it.'

'Find it!' I shouted at the top of my voice. 'I'll find it.' And I set off.

I could see them right from the edge of the roundabout at Elephant. They were even taller than I'd imagined. So tall that I couldn't see where the cranes ended and the sky began. A row of people like ants streamed up them and disappeared. I suspected they should fall like raindrops but they didn't. They just climbed and then disappeared. It would take me an age to get to the top. It would be dark by the time I was up there. Nobody would see me coming and I'd land on someone's head. *Consequence*, I scratched my head in frustration. *The one thing in the world I hate more than anything else is consequence.*

There are processes that take you places in your mind which are like a blanket. A warm, thick blanket that you want to crawl up inside and disappear. Walking is one of them. Your feet thud on the ground and you could be anywhere. London would get to you if you were stood still but when you walk it just vanishes – gone. No traffic; no lorries reversing into your path; no people or anything around and then you find yourself at the cranes. The great big fuckers that scrape the sky. You don't know how you got there but everyone's looking at you and talking at you and asking you questions like: *What's your BMI?*; and *How much training have you done?*; and *Do you realise that it's forty thousand rungs on the ladder before you get to the platform?* And I was there with my head spinning and the world buzzing and all of these weird sights around me. People were praying and hugging and making love in the alleyway. And there was a real edge to proceedings and I didn't say anything but I was suddenly signing a document with a man stood in front of me in a florescent jacket with a yellow hard hat and glasses. He looked down his nose as he leaned in over me. I signed it. Of course I signed it, because he looked official and the pen was in my hand and the ladder was in front of me and I put my hand on the first rung, cold, hard steel and then there was nobody.

The world was quiet and there was a faint mist in the air and I wondered: *Where are all the buildings and the cars? Where are all the people watching?* For a while I just hung there, one rung off the ground, hugging the steel as though my life depended on it. I realised, when I was close up with it pressing against my cheek, that the steel could communicate. It was a real talker in fact. It told me that everything was going to be OK and that I just had to keep climbing and I'd get up to the top. It promised me all sorts of things and they weren't sordid or twisted but clean and pure. It promised me not just alloy but precious metal, the kind that wars are fought for. And I believed everything it told me and I started to climb.

It was hard work. I realised it sooner than I'd hoped. All the while the steel was telling me the things that I wanted to hear: that I was stronger than I thought; that my lungs were clean and my mind was pure. It repeated it to me, like a lullaby, only mechanical, like a robotic woodpecker tapping out Morse code. Underneath its voice there was a long, low murmur, like electricity was running up around me, like some kind of force field. I started to get confused, to become dizzy and it buzzed like a chainsaw, suddenly angry, suddenly trying to push me back down. I felt as though my body was being pushed through an inkjet printer, my life spread out on A3 paper in block print with all of the horrors erased so that I smiled up from the page like a child. It hurt. I held on and closed my eyes. I begged it to stop and it did, leaving me with nothing but a wash like the rush of the sea. Then it went quiet.

'How far up?' I asked it. 'Not far,' it replied, 'but further. Have you seen the view? Take a look. Take a moment and look.'

I held on tighter when I realised just how high I was already. Below me the roofs of London were cobbled together and broken apart into a wandering maze. And I looked down. They always tell you not to look down, so that's exactly what you do. And I saw all of the faces below, turned upwards to the sky and to me on the ladder, willing me to climb higher, to go up and up into the sky. I looked up to try and see where I was aiming for but there was only an endless ladder disappearing into the sun and someone else clinging on above me. He looked weary, more tired than I was. I shouted to him to keep going and he smiled. Then he began to climb, just as a voice from below urged me to do the same and I looked down to see a young woman with her skirt blowing in the breeze and I wished a deep wish that she was above me.

Then as I began to climb I realised that she was and her skirt flitted around revealing flashes of her skin below. I began to climb faster but each time I got close she would continue on a few rungs and get away from me again. All of London was gone now and there was only the girl and a glimpse that I was to search for. So, I climbed and climbed until I saw her reach the top and disappear over the lip of some great steel ledge. I rushed to meet her, to be there with her at the top. But when I got there it was just another ladder: a smaller, more flimsy-looking one, and she was gone – up somewhere into the sky and I knew that I would never catch her.

I turned to look at the world but it was gone too and everything was just blue. Pale, sky blue like a pair of medical scrubs. The wind picked up and it was cold. I felt the platform sway beneath me and I held onto the ladder, pushing the steel close to my face. And it told me things. It told me that I would be safe, if I just held on. It told me that it could bend in the wind and that it would not break. And I believed it. I held it tight and pushed myself into it. And I believed every word.

THE WEDDING PHOTO   KEVIN HALLERAN

It's down here, what we want to show you. Almost buried along the lower row of this temporary wall the workers erected around the site, plastered end to end across the block with pictures and messages, yearbook photos, handmade signs, pillows with stitched initials, newspaper clippings, names written in spray paint or chalk. So many names. After all it wasn't just the people in the towers – there were the passengers on the planes, passers-by on the street, and all the firefighters and rescue workers. All of them are here on the wall now in some form or another. The one we want to show you is down here somewhere. Every time Bonnie and I come it gets harder to find it – new pictures always seem to be appearing. I guess it takes some people longer to say goodbye. Bonnie and I sometimes wonder what will happen when the work is finished and the wall is taken down. Where will they all go?

Here it is, near the bottom like I told you. Go ahead and take a seat on the sidewalk. Here they are: the bride and groom. Look how young. What would you say – twenty-two for her and twenty-three for him? That's what we came up with. Look how proud and perfect her smile is, like the braces just came off yesterday. And him, even the retouching on this photo can't airbrush all the pimples off his face. That's why this picture stood out to us among all the others. Look how young, I said to Bonnie the first time. Then in unison we said, High school sweethearts. Know why we're so sure? Look how comfortable they are with each other. Her head tilts against his shoulder so those blonde curls drape over the front of his tuxedo, yet she's careful not to cover any of his face; and he's clearly much taller than her but bends over slightly to make them appear more equal. This isn't the first time they've posed together for a picture. Homecoming, prom, graduation, you name it – they were old pros at it by now.

Although she did turn him down the first time he asked her out.

Yes, of course she did. With her marble blue eyes she had her pick of the school. But he was persistent and clever. He used that sly grin and sense of humour to make impressions on her friends and got them to win her over for him. Then, believe it or not, they split up after high school. She went off to school in Rhode Island and he did community college while working at his father's store. Neither wanted the other to feel tied down and resentful, so they agreed to see other people but of course neither one did. They both stayed home at night listening to Van Morrison and wondering what the other was doing. After a year he transferred to her school and that was it. They thought about staying in Rhode Island after graduation but the work just wasn't there, so they came back home. She worked for an investment firm (such an intelligent-looking face). We're not positive what he did, but Bonnie swears it was something technical. It's his fingers, she says, the way they wrap around hers so nimbly. Electrician or computer repair – someone used to handling delicate things.

At first we didn't know they both worked here in the towers. We thought they were on one of the planes heading for their honeymoon (Hawaii – both have such fair skin that they desperately needed some sun), but then we realised they couldn't have afforded it since they were saving for a house in Westchester. They wanted to move out of their little one-bedroom downtown as soon as possible and start a family. Two girls and a boy was what they were shooting for. Two girls and a boy would have been so nice, wouldn't it?

Naturally, they had their problems too. Every young couple does. They were both working so hard they didn't have much time for each other, and contrary to what you might have heard, when you're young absence only makes the heart grow bitter. They began to fight over the dumbest things – whose turn it was to pick up the dry cleaning, or why the orange juice had pulp – but after a while even the little things add up and nothing seems trivial anymore.

Did they fight that morning? What did they see the last time their eyes met? Was it the couple in this photo or someone else? Bonnie

35

and I disagree on this. She says that their little tiffs were always resolved by the time they went to bed. They were more in love than ever that morning, she says, and they thought of nothing but each other when the final moment came. But I say the reason someone chose to memorialise them this way, with this picture, is because they wanted to recall a happier time in their life, a time that was long gone and unrecoverable. No one wants them to be remembered as they actually were that day, run down and hardened, young in age but weathered in spirit. Instead we are asked to remember them at their best, to preserve a love as it once was and always should have been, which is the least any of us can do for someone. That's what Bonnie and I are here for. Maybe somebody will do the same for us.

John lay on soiled sheets like a done, old dog on an acrid blanket. He remembered peeing himself as a child, awakening to the long, warm flow. Now it alarmed him that it was expected again as he could feel the slip of a waterproof under the hospital bedclothes.

He looked to the bedside locker; the buzzer was gone, and he needed to shout for help. Damn it all, because Derek was visiting soon.

Madge's flowers were still on the locker, they irritated the hell out of him with their sunshine, yellow cheeriness over a red, plastic bow. 'From Madge with love': huh, and pity for the coronary victim. At least she'd delivered them personally along with unsolicited advice about Derek, but she'd brought grapes though she knew he'd prefer sweets. Hell, why did he care anyway? He was a crippled, old widower, semi-incontinent, with an interfering sister and an estranged son. Madge had probably told Derek he was dying, that would explain his visit.

John squealed out in a voice barely familiar to him like an old woman's cry. A nurse came in, she was brisk but cheerful. Now he'd be washed. What's left to a person who can't even bathe himself anymore?

'We'll have you right as rain in no time,' the nurse explained, 'ready to see your son.'

God, Madge must have told everyone about his visitor.

'What were you thinking? Nothing clean to wear in the house, and the state of the place – what if you'd died?' Madge had complained. Then she bought him new pyjamas, and the contents of his soap bag. Jesus, now they'd wash him with her leavings. He'd smell of her damned, perfumed soap.

The nurse left the room, returning a few minutes later with a male nurse and a wheelchair. They peeled back the sodden bedclothes. John closed his eyes and tried to think of a distraction, but it didn't help. So he opened his eyes and watched them work. They removed the sheets and his pyjama trousers, the male nurse wiping him down; he was gentle and professional, avoiding John's gaze, like an undertaker washing a corpse. Then they turned John over to wash him underneath, patting him dry, extra careful in the creases of his skin.

'We don't want you smarting, John, now do we?'

'I did this for Derek once, a long time ago,' said John.

'Derek?' asked the male nurse.

'He's my only child, and he was ill at the time. My wife offered, but a grown man is heavy.'

'I'm sorry about that. Did he get well again?'

'Yes, I suppose so. I don't see much of him since my wife died, but he is coming to see me this afternoon.'

'Right then, we'll get you all comfortable for Derek coming.'

They lifted him into the wheelchair to bring him to the bathroom.

Back then, John had noticed the bruising first: black and purple patches on the chest, yellowed where Derek was healing. Those thugs had done a proper job on him. At least his face was saved where he'd squeezed it into his forearms and curled from their kicks. John propped up his son with pillows and began to ease off his pyjamas. Derek looked feeble and shaken, wrung out with pain.

'Hang on, son, don't move. I'll get the basin and cloth; I've made sure the water's nice and warm.'

'Don't worry, Da. I'm not going anywhere.'

'It's only a turn of phrase, son.'

'Yes, like "normal" I suppose.'

John made no answer. He'd got used to the surly remarks. But why couldn't the boy have gone to normal clubs?

He continued to undress Derek, raising each arm in turn, removing his pyjama top. He folded it with care and set it aside.

'I used to bath you when you were a wee boy. Do you remember? You liked me to help you.'

'And I thought that was Ma's job... I don't want to trouble you, you know. I'll be gone as soon as I'm well.'

'That's not what I want, son. This is your home. But you know how hard this is on your mother.' John leaned across and pulled down Derek's pyjama bottoms. The bruising was worse around the top of his thighs; it was hard to look at. There had been four of them at him, pulling him straight to kick at his groin.

'It's looking better,' remarked Derek, 'I can pee by myself now, even if it is into a bottle.'

John washed his son in gentle strokes careful of the bruising. But Derek closed his eyes, and John had to turn from him. This frail, young man was his boy: face thin and pale, bruises blotted a slight frame. John was afraid for his son; he had to steel himself to complete the task.

'For God's sake, why did you put yourself in the way of this?' asked John, as he drew the sheet up again. Then he turned and left the room.

Derek was sitting waiting when John was wheeled back from the bathroom. John stiffened in panic as the nurses lifted him from the wheelchair and placed him onto the bed. He reached for the bedclothes but his grip was too feeble and they tucked him in too tightly.

'Thank you,' he said. Then he faced his son. 'Hello, Derek. How are you?' The boy looked older than he remembered.

'I'm fine, Da – you don't look great.'

'Yes, don't feel too good either. Any news from the city?'

Derek stood up and walked towards the window. There was nothing much out there to look at, but he lingered for a moment before he answered.

'Eh... I got promoted and bought a new apartment. It's a lovely spot overlooking the river.'

'Is *he* living there too?' asked John.

'You mean Terry? Of course he is. We're still together, Da.' Derek sighed.

John was distressed now, though he didn't show it. Try again, he thought, say something nice to him even if you don't mean it.

'Did you come straight from work? Your mother always loved to see you in a suit and tie. She was better at news.'

'Yeah, Da, I miss her.'

'So do I, son. But she went quickly... didn't suffer.' Then John changed the subject and they settled into some small talk of neighbours and cousins. Derek sat down again.

The visitors' bell rang, and Derek straightened in his chair. He clasped his hands together and John knew the gesture – the boy was nervous.

'Da, there's something we need to talk about before I go.'

'What's that, son?'

'I know that you can't look after yourself. You're going to need help.'

John stiffened in the bed.

'Right, so that's why you're here. I don't need your help, son.'

'Yes you do, Da. I've talked to the doctor.'

So, they'd been talking about him, making decisions. Madge had started this, discussing his future and how to manage him.

'I'm not helpless, you know, just cos I can't wash myself.'

'Yes, Da, I know. You know well I do. That's why I came, to find out what you want. But Madge isn't fit to care for you.'

'MADGE, she'd have me dead in a week.'

Then Derek started wittering on about how John couldn't live alone, or God forbid, come and stay with him. But John didn't want to live with anyone. He was tired, and he recognised that familiar drag – the twist and strain of mutual disappointment.

'Da, you mightn't have much choice about this,' Derek urged. He was firm, and John was frightened now. He struggled to straighten himself, as if that might prove something, but he couldn't lean forward and Derek had to help.

'I want to go home, son. I want to be in my own house, and die in my own bed.'

'Nobody's talking about dying; you just need a hand for a while.

Content yourself, Da. We'll sort something out.'

John tried to sit upright. Derek moved forward, and helped to raise him further up in the bed. The old man complied as he was lifted, and his pillows fluffed.

'You don't understand, son, I need to go home.' John couldn't stand the hospital, every room smelled the same.

'Calm yourself, Da.'

'Calm myself? Son, I can't picture your mum's face anymore. I don't see her, even when I close my eyes.'

But Derek gave off that John was too worked up. If only he would relax and let *him* sort things out. He had money now and could pay for a nice place – he even had somewhere in mind.

'Son,' said John, 'if I die, will you wake me in my own house?'

Derek didn't reply. But John knew what his son saw: his unkempt hair and the fragile skin sunken at the cheeks, his narrowed shoulders, scrawny hands and the long, bony thighs deep in the blankets. He tried again.

'Please, son. Would you promise me? You can bury me in orange boxes for all I care, but I want to be waked in my own home... not one of those funeral parlours like an auld one with no-one belonging to him.'

'At your house, like we did for Ma?'

That was the last time John had seen Derek. He had left with his mother's coffin.

Derek stood, and started to waffle on again. This time it was about going, and being back in the morning. But he still didn't answer the question. John listened for it. Then he left the room, and John watched him retreat. He noticed that Derek's hair was greying at the back, but his shoulders were still fine and broad under his suit. The boy might have been a footballer once, a county player even. He could have made it too, if only he'd put in the right kind of effort when it really mattered.

John wouldn't give up; he'd work on Derek about a proper wake. There was still enough time to change the boy's mind.

LILETTE SPEAKS FRENCH   CLAIRR O'CONNOR

Lilette doesn't like to point out that her husband is driving down the wrong side of the road. They are abroad. Abroad makes him nervous. He rarely goes there. This is abroad with a foreign language. A first, for Feargal. She doesn't want to provoke a row. It has taken decades for him to take this journey with her.

After a couple of outraged horn-blasts from other drivers he is back on course again after some muttered indignation. They are in Cannes, courtesy of St Jude's, the convent she had taught French in for thirty years. At fifty two, she has taken early retirement. The staff has given her the trip as a present.

She'd fallen in love with the sound of French even before she could speak it. When she was a student at St Jude's herself, she was taught by Sister Marguerite, a Parisian who started each day with, 'Bonjour, mes enfants.' Lilette felt herself glow in Sister Marguerite's class. She gave all the children French versions of their names. Lily became Lilette and she loved it so much when she went home she insisted her parents adopt the French version of her name.

Sometimes she wonders how she could have married Feargal two decades ago? His refusal of a Paris honeymoon, compliments of her great-aunt, should have been warning enough. But she had a physical passion for him that has lasted to this day. Love makes you weak. She hadn't wanted to marry anyone but succumbed to Feargal's pleas when she was thirty two on certain conditions – that she would continue to teach at St Jude's and that she would retain her long-established practice of having a month's holiday in France each year. He agreed, convinced that the charms of life on the farm and children would be enough for her.

After two years and two babies, she thought she would die of exhaustion. He thought she would resign from St Jude's. Instead, she swallowed the pill secretly and took the children to France each summer when school closed.

Lilette and Feargal are now on the way to the supermarket. They are spending two weeks in a high-rise apartment in Cannes. Lilette has arranged it through a French friend who teaches in the Lycèe Carnot. Feargal, used to the farmhouse and hundreds of acres around him, can't adjust to the noise of dogs barking in the neighbourhood, let alone the proximity of the neighbours themselves.

'Why aren't they on their holidays?' he remarks, stricken, on their first night.

'Because they live here and they can't all be on holiday just because it's summer,' Lilette says with the professional patience of the teacher.

If he is going to be intolerant, she would simply have to tune it out. This was his first time in France with her. Some of his cronies in Walsh's pub had mocked him that Lilette was always going abroad alone and this sorry situation was the result. Feargal finally parks their hired car, almost scraping another one.

In the supermarket Lilette dances along the aisles putting treats as well as necessities into the shopping cart. Feargal trails behind. He seems stunned that all the labels are actually in French.

'Bread?' he snaps, as she approaches the cashier.

'No need, there's a boulangerie in our block.'

'You know I don't drink wine,' he says, looking at the six bottles in the cart.

'Not to worry, they're for me and my friends.'

The next day, they are to tour a perfume factory in Grasse and visit the Provençal costume museum. Afterwards, they will lunch with her friend Clothilde. She's an artist with an atelier in the old city. Feargal gets hopelessly lost on the way there. She remains mute while he fumes. Eventually, he relinquishes the wheel and they're in Grasse very quickly once Lilette gets on the right motorway.

The tour guide in the factory is a stunner. She's early twenties, model thin, and dressed in a black suit. All the men are enthralled. Feargal loses his prescription sunglasses, only realising it after the tour finishes. The mademoiselle magicks them up for him and he blushes when he tips her.

Clothilde is delighted to see Lilette and is prepared to include Feargal. She does not believe in pandering to men and has dismissed her latest lover, fifteen years her junior, that week. They have an agreeable lunch at an open-air café and Feargal decides to do a walking tour of Grasse because he takes an instant dislike to Clothilde. He considers her rude and complains on the journey back to the apartment. Lilette tells him to concentrate on the road or they'll get lost.

A routine begins to assert itself. They swim in the very early morning when the beach is quiet. The exercise makes them competitive as they swim out to sea in noisy playfulness. Their high spirits last over breakfast and a walk in the nearby park. On the way back they buy bread. Feargal goes to an Irish pub for lunch where he enjoys the release of speaking English. He's making little progress with the survival French phrases booklet that Lilette gave him. She has never encountered such a resistant student. She spends the afternoons in a gallery or museum and they meet again for dinner. Some nights they eat at the local brasserie, Lilette ordering for both of them. Feargal usually has a meat dish. They have fish and salad on the nights they're in. It's quick and there's a great variety of fish available.

He tells her stories about the people from the pub. According to Feargal, most of the unfortunate Irish who are regulars came to the south of France to work during the blighted eighties in Ireland. A minority followed the women they loved and now their children were French. Lilette gives edited versions of her outings with her friend Clothilde to see this or that exhibition.

She attempts to explain him to Clothilde. What a charmer he is at home in his own environment. Being abroad makes him insecure and obstinate. He misses the farm. The only holidays he's had, by choice, are two weeks in Ballybunion with Lilette and the children, Ballybunion being the nearest seaside resort to the farm. He could nip back for a few hours in the evening to check that Mattie, the farm manager, had everything under control.

Their final week is to be spent at St-Paul-de-Vence at the beautiful hotel, La Colombe d'Or. Lilette does not tell Feargal the enormous expense of the place or that she has saved a long time for this luxury week and booked a year in advance. Instead she tells him that they are going to a beautiful fortified town way up in the mountains with a watchtower from the twelfth century and that the first owner of the hotel was a farmer called Paul Roux.

She spends the day before they leave Cannes patiently marking the route on the map and deconstructing the mystery of road signs for Feargal. He now knows that 'cedez le passage' means give way. That evening she checks and packs the formal clothes that they haven't worn in Cannes.

'It's fancy, then,' he says, noting her efforts.

'A little,' she says.

He drives the route beautifully and is consequently in good form when they arrive. She hands her most coveted piece of pigskin luggage to the porter and he smiles. Finally, getting through the wooden door to the Colombe d'Or from the square has made her giddy even before she sees their room. She is delighted to see so much art casually displayed. She notes a Picasso, a Leger and a Bonnard. Their room is a delight. It has a high bed with a sturdy stool to help the ascent, a massive wardrobe and shuttered windows. It overlooks the terrace. The en-suite bathroom is generous, with fittings of old marble.

That evening, Feargal eats too many hors d'oeuvres from an enormous platter and leaves half his veal from the main course. They share a sorbet for dessert. There is a Braque and Dufy on their side of the dining room. Coffee is taken on the terrace looking at the fading light and later they make love in the big bed, their first time on this holiday. Not even the mosquitoes buzzing through the open shutters bother them.

Next day, they climb the winding streets of the village and walk along the ramparts. Afterwards, they stop at a café for coffee in the square and meet an Irish couple, the Kennedys from Wexford, on holiday also. He's an engineer and she's a civil servant, both in their mid forties. By the second coffee, Feargal is suggesting they meet for dinner that evening. They eat at the Ste Claire, which is a little outside St-Paul. It's a noisy evening where food and drink are consumed apace without much consideration by Feargal and his new friends. Lilette feels she's the outsider.

The Kennedys become the focus of Feargal's attention during their stay.

'What's the attraction?' Lilette enquires.

'They speak English,' Feargal says.

Lilette insists they have dinner every second evening at La Colombe d'Or. It's obvious that Feargal enjoys the more gregarious evenings with the Kennedys at the Ste Claire and their evenings on their own have taken on something of the punitive from Feargal's point of view.

'Nobody speaks English at our hotel,' he had confided to the Kennedys that first evening, 'except this American couple, the Marlows. They're art collectors.'

Lilette had spent a lovely morning with the Marlows at the Maeght Foundation admiring Miro's Labyrinth and an afternoon at Matisse's Chapelle du Rosaire at Vence.

Before this trip it had troubled her how she was going to tell Feargal of her future plans to spend more time in France now that she was no longer teaching. At first, she thought she would wait until they went back home to Ireland but by their second week at La Colombe d'Or even she dreaded the evening meal. It was 'sinful' to charge so much for food, Feargal opined, even though Lilette reminded him he wasn't paying for it. Each of his critiques depressed her. She had spent twenty years living on a farm with him when an urban way of life would have suited her interests better.

She had tried over the years to get him interested in France and to holiday with her and the children but he had refused. Fifteen years ago the apartment next to Clothilde's was for sale and she had urged Lilette to buy it. It was reasonably priced and had two bedrooms. When Lilette was marrying Feargal, her great-aunt Hanora gave her a set of beautiful pigskin luggage and this advice, 'Remember, everything will be alright as long as you have your glad money.' Glad money was the money you saved every month that you didn't tell anyone about. The advice stuck. Lilette put some money away each month in good times and bad. That was how she had enough for a deposit and regular mortgage repayments if she could sublet. Clothilde said she could arrange short-term lets for her when she wasn't there. All these years Feargal had assumed she was subletting from Clothilde.

Lilette loved her students. They called her Madame. She was going to miss them terribly. At dinner, on the terrace of the Ste Claire she told Feargal and the Kennedys about her plans to spend more time in the apartment in Grasse. Their two children, Mathew and Maeve, were in college in Dublin, both studying French and History. She imagined they would spend long holidays with her there. Finally, she had Feargal's attention.

AT THE MONTBELIARD STATION   NIGEL JARRETT

Perhaps the train slowed for the driver to see what was going on, because it was not scheduled to stop. A commuter lay on his back while five or six members of his tribe knelt beside him, their rolled umbrellas criss-crossed on the platform, their briefcases piled like votive offerings. The scene slid past. Then the train picked up speed and was soon among meadows again, the distant farmhouses and their bow-backed occupants restoring a feeling of comfortable ease.

'You never actually see it,' the archbishop said, forming a pyramid with his outstretched fingers. 'Considering how many of us are supposed to be falling like flies, the chances of our witnessing a heart attack must be pretty high. But it usually happens elsewhere, among others. We sometimes have to will it.'

Michael, the archbishop's secretary, made no reply to a statement which required none, apart from a possible rebuttal. To a wider public, the archbishop had probably made his final *ex cathedra* judgement. The archbishop himself knew this, which was why his right hand dropped gently on to his secretary's and was held there for longer than the other passengers might have considered discreet. An indiscretion having been perpetrated, the pyramid was re-built.

Archbishop Summoned To Vatican – the newspaper headlines had ushered the pair of them on to the railway station at home, with reporters and photographers in scuffing pursuit. They had out-distanced them in a bracing atmosphere of notoriety, which, in the secretary's case, was short-lived. Now, the Alps were coming into view as the train rounded a bend among trees. Later, as the much-travelled Michael knew, the land would unaccountably level out and the train would cross the unending lowlands of the poor.

'Don't you think, Michael, that the Primate, God bless his soul, might be slightly envious of us at this precise moment?'

'Perhaps. But only at this precise moment. The Primate sees

farther ahead.'

'Ah! How we have prided ourselves on being able to know what is around the next corner. That's the trouble with Fate – it takes all the excitement out of life.'

Through Calais, Paris, Dijon and Lyon, the secretary had tried to imagine what lay ahead: a meeting with high-ranking Papal emissaries possibly, or a nominal rebuke from a cleric at the end of a corridor. The picture had so far eluded him. For some reason he set to thinking about a passage from St Augustine in which demonic miracles, such as the scooping of Tiber water into a sieve by a vestal virgin suspected of transgressing her vows, are compared to the grand and powerful ones performed among the people of God. The archbishop was fixated by miracles and their authenticity – once, as a country priest on a coach trip to Lourdes, he had become famously tipsy. The Church had insisted on their flying to Rome; but the archbishop had negotiated a compromise: a slower, contemplative journey out and a return by air. The Primate had nodded his assent. Michael – devoted Michael Donnelly O'Touhig – had made the arrangements.

For an hour the train seemed to meander at leisure, so that the sun's rays played intermittently on the archbishop's brow, stretching his lips into what could have been either a smile or a faint grimace. Half asleep, he asked: 'What was that place, the one with the corpse?'

'We don't know he was dead,' the secretary replied, as though the doubt had some bearing on the answer to the question. With a long, pendulous finger, he checked the name on the map. 'Montbeliard,' he said, looking back at the landscape they had passed through. He had been recommended to the archbishopric as 'scrupulous', a quality which the scandals had brought out; in fact, his devotion to a sometimes trying, unconventional man had always made it essential. Montbeliard and its significance led nowhere.

'What will you do, Michael, if it goes against me?'

'What will *you* do?'

The archbishop frowned at this stalling. A more impatient man would have thought it impertinent. Yet this was all he had left, this pretence.

'Let's wait and see what happens.'

The secretary hoped that everything would turn out well for the archbishop. Retirement would not be unproductive or even laden with remorse. There was even talk of his being recruited by the television people as a celebrity. After all, his sin was one of omission and, following a lifetime of venial controversy, forgiveness would be unofficial but widespread. But where had he been when Father Julius's marble-cold palm closed on the choirboy's knee or the sweet lips of Mary Flaherty puckered as she gripped the back of O'Rourke's thighs? And what of old Cotter, moved by the bishop from parish to parish as though a change of air would stifle his roguery? On the subject of wickedness the Church was supposed to be adamant; where depravity was concerned it was expected to be militant. But the archbishop believed in the triumph of shame, however long deferred. It was a belief consonant with ruddy cheeks, a raucous laugh and a passion for swirling, Herebus-dark stout.

Rome assailed them. It wasn't just the heat but the ricochet of heat off stone and water that slowed their pace. They shielded their eyes. In St Peter's, they sought the shadows like a pair of conspirators. Michael was conducting yet another tedious rehearsal, unheard among the multitudes.

'I cannot plead innocence. Michael,' the archbishop said. 'That would mean admitting dereliction of duty. I have to agree that mistakes have been made and be passionate about not wishing to repeat them. We've gone through all this.'

'Yes we have. And we know that our record – your record – suggests that mistakes are being multiplied. I don't know what their reaction will be to that.'

This was pitiless. The older man gripped the back of the chair in front and looked forlornly at the drifting crowds. He always had a high colour but now it seemed to have spread. Michael noticed this and also glimpsed how the archbishop's recent loss of weight had opened up a gap between neck and collar. Inside the collar lay the patterned grime of travel. The archbishop had been pressed for his story but he wanted Michael to write something more formal, a biography no less, that might make of ignominy, regrettable though it was, a mere addendum to a life of service. Michael had shrugged assent, a sure sign that the job would be done. Photographic albums had been plundered and illustrations chosen. The archbishop particularly liked the one of the seminary graduation class, that wave of rectitude consisting of piled-up ranks of apostles, anonymous and undivided. Michael had smiled at the possibility of having to encircle the archbishop's head with a white, identifying halo.

Outside the Vatican, they met the man from the BBC, who spoke for a slouch of other journalists and photographers. The heat seemed to have got to them too. But among the shoals of worshippers in the square, even an archbishop and his personal secretary were reduced to small fry. To the archbishop, this indicated the ascension of divine authority and the humility of the righteous, and he suddenly felt jaunty, a word often used to describe him by fellow 'Rock Cakes' in less reverent mood. The Primate had insisted on Michael's reading a prepared statement after the hearing and had told him there was no need to phone with the outcome.

A preliminary meeting attended by Michael preceded the one from which he was excluded – the archbishop's interrogation by a committee of three. Michael waited in an ante-room, then spent a while in the corridor, leaning against a cool marble column. He had a momentary craving for a cigarette. (Old Cotter smoked so heavily that he could remove the carbon stains from his fingers but not the honeyed yellow veil left after much scrubbing.) A party of elderly Japanese glided past, accompanied by two Papal officials, one of them taking particular care of its oldest member, a man not walking fast enough even for the air to disturb a wispy grey beard. The Pope was in South America, giving succour to the poor while protected by glass from the passion of the gun-toting AntiChrist. Michael and the archbishop often joked about their Church and its sometimes obtuse leader. He looked around him and listened. Ardour and ecstasy were subsumed there, dignified by authority and the silent emptiness of removal and distance. Perhaps if he bought a pack of cigarettes, the archbishop would join him later in a triumphant drag on a park bench. Any result would be worth celebrating.

'As we thought, Michael,' the archbishop said, after striding jauntily down the corridor. 'A year or two of grace, during which we rid ourselves of our unfortunate canker, followed by my retirement on grounds to be mutually agreed. But we'll keep the last bit quiet.'

There was a TV camera on them as Michael read a statement which did not apportion blame but emphasised Rome's commitment to ridding the Church of 'insidious evils'. Michael found out by phone that none of the Italian pictures of them were televised in Britain, only worn-out footage of Father Julius winning the egg-and-spoon race at the St Gabriel's bazaar and the still photograph of O'Rourke from police files with its expression wavering between guilt and penitence. Old Cotter had only ever been mentioned in passing, his actions more comical than venial.

After dinner, they worked out what to say to the *Morning Post*, the local daily back home with the insolent 'Proddy' reporter, and considered the reams of stuff that would no doubt be demanded by the *Herald*. Regional TV would require the archbishop to speak to camera while its report intoned piously above the once-more athletic Julius, the Mafioso O'Rourke and – just maybe – that picture of a much younger Cotter which had given the old reprobate immunity by deception.

Still, Michael knew that Cotter would have to be contacted. They all would – Julius at the Priory, O'Rourke in jail and even crafty Bill Leonard, their self-appointed 'Devil's Disciple', not the latest to join but by far the most outspoken opponent of the 'ring', as the hounding press always referred to them. The ring to which, of course, he belonged. The trouble with loners, in this as in the priesthood, was the risk of apostasy followed by contrition in public, behaviour not far removed from what was now laughingly called 'whistle-blowing': whistling that theme from Elgar's *The Dream of Gerontius* (a setting of Cardinal Newman, they always reminded themselves) was the secret phone code that alerted them to new vistas, to the dancing circle of the innocents (some not so bloody innocent, Bill Leonard said). He still remembered how it quickened his heartbeat when he heard it before anyone spoke down the wire and how it sealed their conclave from interference.

Michael drew heavily on his cigarette at the open window now that the archbishop had turned in. He could hear the old man snoring and talking gibberish in his sleep. Outside, the electric night flickered above floodlit fountains. He smiled on recalling the tone-deaf Cotter's inability to whistle anything in tune.

But Cotter himself would already be half-asleep among the mountains of Derrynane, where there was scarcely a modern telephone exchange let alone images set in beguiling phosphorescence on a screen. (The idea of it – old Cotter illuminated in ecstasy, like a scoutmaster peering into a tent full of boys around a hurricane lamp!) As the mists dropped for an eternity on Dun Geagan like a benediction, Cotter had moved on beyond any prospect of taking fright at what the wider world was telling him.

'Praise to the holiest for that,' Michael whispered. '*Se vuoi, puniscimi – ma pria, Signore, lascia che almeno sfoghi, che almeno pria si moderi, il tuo sdegno, il tuo furore.*'

APPARATCHIK   T. N. TREANOR

Beep, beep, beep, beep.

Treasa woke, disorientated, a tightness in her stomach.

Beep, beep, beep, beep.

The room was unfamiliar and too hot. She looked at the pager, winking on the bedside cabinet. In that instant, she loathed its necessity, its purpose.

Beep, beep, beep, beep.

'Fuck it,' she mumbled to herself, regretting it immediately, remembering her promise to her mother to cut down on her cursing.

Beep, beep ...

She pressed the 'off' button and turned on the lamp. Some light showed through the curtain. She turned over her watch. 4.30 am.

'What does he want now?'

Treasa slipped into the bathroom to pee, the extractor fan churning as she turned on the light, certainly loud enough to wake any guests in the adjacent rooms.

Beep, beep, beep, beep.

She pulled up her knickers and went back into the bedroom without washing her hands and turned off the pager once more. She dialled the Minister's room number, but there was no answer. Fully awake now and focussing on not cursing out loud, she searched her handbag for her mobile. She turned it on, and dialled #1.

Call unavailable.

She puzzled for a moment, and then remembered she would have to use the international dialling code.

Beep, beep, beep, beep.

'Shut up,' she called as she turned the pager off again. At the same time, she realised that he must be in some trouble. Still, she dialled reluctantly.

'You took your time.'

She contemplated saying 'sorry', it doing so only seemed to invite invective.

'What's the matter?'

'I'm in fucking hospital, that's what's the matter.'

'Shit. What happened?'

'No time for that, I want you to bring my things.'

'Where's Stephen?'

'Fuck Stephen, riding some Yankee tart, no doubt.'

Doubt it, thought Treasa. She calmed him down and got him to explain which hospital he was in and what he needed. She phoned reception and arranged to get into his room and book a cab to the hospital. She looked longingly at the warm bed, but got into the shower instead.

The hospital was more formal and efficient than any Irish version she had experienced. She sat in the waiting room with the small travel bag on the seat beside her. It contained his VHI documents, a pair of unused pyjamas, a wash bag, a small bottle of hair dye ensconced in the side pocket and his pocket diary. A Latino gentleman was the only other person waiting. The receptionist was Oriental, Chinese probably, but she spoke perfect American. A black woman came in to sweep the floor. She chatted heartily to the receptionist, defying the early hour. Treasa recalled the concern of the Minister the previous evening, about flying back. His normal bravado had dissipated and he was worried. She'd left him at about, well, half eleven, she guessed. Stephen hadn't been seen since dinner, said he was heading out to meet some relatives. The Minister had become horribly maudlin, and Treasa cut her losses and went to bed. Even now, Stephen still had his mobile turned off. She'd texted him, wherever he was, so at least he'd get the message.

'Miss, your father is able to see you now,' called the receptionist.

'He's not my father, he's my employer,' retorted Treasa, quickly. The receptionist arched her eyebrows. Treasa followed her down a corridor and then the receptionist used a pass card to get into the clinical area. A nurse in scrubs took Treasa to the final cubicle. It was neat and organised. The Minister was sitting up on a trolley, his left leg extended with weights hanging off it. He had an IV and was wearing only a paper gown, slack around his shoulders. Treasa thought he looked rough enough, but he gave her his best charming smile. Perhaps because of his surroundings, he couldn't but look like a countryman, helpless in an environment he couldn't control.

'Well, see what I've gone and done to meself?'

Treasa located a small stool and sat beside the trolley. He seemed unnaturally joyous, and she guessed that he'd had some pain killers.

'What have you done?' she asked at last.

He smiled again. 'Fell down the stairs. In the hotel.'

'In the hotel? It's a wonder they never said anything to me.'

'Well, not *our* hotel. I went out for a couple of drinks...'

He blushed a little. She had known him for fifteen years, and had worked for him for eight and had never seen him blush. He returned to his smile.

'Have you told Angela? Or the boss?' she asked.

'Jaysus, no. I thought I'd wait for yourself and Stephen before I did anything. Where is the bollocks, by the way?'

'Fu... Don't know. I've texted him. He'll be along, I'm sure.'

'Little gobshite, can't be relied on, should have let him go years ago. Anyhow, we'll have to manage this somehow.'

Treasa looked about her as if searching for inspiration. A small lady was attending to an old man in a trolley which was at an angle to their own. Clever, the layout. No-one could see another person with any ease. There was a calm that she didn't associate with the EDs in Ireland.

'Well, what's wrong with you?'

He looked at her scornfully. 'I got stung by a bee. What does it look like? I've broken me fucking leg! Fuck's sake, thank God you're not in medicine!'

He relented quickly, touching the back of her hand, the closest he ever came to an apology.

'I was wondering what the plan was. I mean, are they going to operate, can you go home, that sort of thing?'

'Ach, I'd say I'll be here for a good while.' He seemed cheerful about the prospect. 'I won't be setting foot in Ireland for a few weeks yet. What story do we give?'

'To the press or to the boss?'

'Both. I can't be saying that I fell down the stairs of a hotel lobby while half-cut.'

'Well, what did happen?'

'I was half-cut and fell down the stairs of a hotel.' He laughed.

Treasa didn't like this sort of work. Nappy work, she called it, not what she thought she'd signed up for.

'I mean, were there witnesses, who took you to hospital, which hotel was it? I mean, what do we know and what can we control?'

'Fuck all, I'd say. I'm not sure of the hotel. Witnesses... none I'd care to name. The doorman called the ambulance, I think. Sure, I didn't even get inside...'

'It was on the street?'

'Aye, where did you think it was?'

Treasa had imagined him upstairs in some bordello.

'Right. We'll just say that you fell down, broke your leg, on some steps. We say you were taken to the hospital, and we are awaiting the results of tests, but that you may be incapacitated for some time.'

'At three in the morning?'

'We don't say the time. We can say you were admitted on Sunday morning.'

'And we tell that to everybody?'

'Everybody. Is anybody likely to contradict us?'

The Minister thought briefly, and then winced as he tried to relieve the pressure on his backside and move himself up the trolley. 'No, I don't think so.'

Treasa stifled a yawn. She wanted to go back to bed. She wanted to go home. She wished she could just be there, not have to endure the red-eye or be back working in Dublin on Monday afternoon. She tried to think where she'd rather be; a beach, a cool wind, but her inability to be more specific disturbed her. She handed over the wash bag, and watched as the Minister combed his hair and checked his teeth.

'I could do with a shave,' he said, rubbing his palm across his bristly jowls. He looked up at her. 'Thank you.'

Treasa was just getting back into bed, when Stephen called on the internal phone.

'Where were you?'

'No matter. I got your text. Is he okay?'

Treasa thought. 'Yeah. More than okay. Unnaturally happy. I haven't seen him like that for ages. Drug-induced, I reckon. Where are you?'

'In my room.'

'Well, we're going to be here for another wee while. That a problem for you?'

Silence.

'Fair enough, so. I'm going to try and get some sleep.'

'Good idea. You were up early, I heard.'

He heard?

'Flip it, Stephen, we'll meet up, have a coffee or something.'

'I can't do this shite anymore.'

Treasa didn't want to hear it. She wanted to have said it first, and now she felt as if it were a betrayal.

'He's changed...'

Stephen didn't have to tell her. Her mother loved the idea of what she did. Ministerial aide. She loved the idea herself. The practicality was different. One of the cleverest men she had ever met. Clever, yes, she conceded, but not intelligent. He could get things done, but it was clear to her now, had been clear for a while, that he had no idea of *what* had to be done. Neither did she. Just do the job, tidy the mess, prepare the briefing, tell Angela I'm working...

He'd made a play for her once. Seven years ago. In Wexford. Another hotel. Drink had been taken, that was a given. He'd kissed her. She had let him. It was going to happen. And then they stopped. He'd said the right things. 'Twouldn't be right, wrong time, only for Angela, don't mix work and play. She respected him for that. She'd comforted herself that the desire was there, but that circumstances... She realised now that, by doing what he'd done, he had more of a hold on her than if nothing had happened, or indeed if they had gone all the way. That slyness. Wily enough to keep her hanging on for six, seven more years. He knew she was practical, could do things. She looked good, as long as she took the lower step, didn't stand above him, didn't mention the hair, or the drinking. But he'd planned it, kept her strung along. Never made another move. Always 'respected' her. Stephen was still talking.

'... and so that was it, he threw himself off of the steps, full drunk.'

'I'm sorry, Stephen, what are you saying?'

'What?'

'You think he did it deliberately?'

'That's what I'm saying, he doesn't want to go home, not yet, he's afeared he'll be injuncted or subpoenaed or something.'

Treasa paused. 'And so he threw himself down some steps?'

'Well, a lot of steps actually. If he'd landed any other way, he could be in a worse state, killed himself or something.'

'That boy! That boy! He'll always land the right flipping way! How do you know all this anyhow?'

A pause.

'What about this coffee?'

Treasa doubted if she would really hear the truth anyway.

'Ah no. I think I'll take a nap like I said. We'll meet later and call in to himself.'

Stephen sounded regretful. 'Right so... sleep well.'

Treasa put the phone down, and pulled the bedclothes over her.

Beep, beep, beep, beep.

Treasa hit the 'off' button and went into the bathroom. She filled the basin with water and placed the pager at the bottom. She dried her hands and returned to bed. She could hear the sounds of the city like a TV soundtrack as she drifted off to sleep.

THE SONG   CONOR MCMANUS

That Sunday afternoon somebody's golden Labrador retriever with a brown collar was jumping up at the window in the kitchen, trying to eat a bluebottle. Growling, with head lowered, the dog would step back, then pounce at the window open mouthed. With his paws on the low sill he'd snap sideways at the fly buzzing and banging off the glass. Music was coming from the front bar and the potatoes were boiling on the back ring.

Joe Galvin was standing at the cooker with a cigarette dangling from his mouth, bodhrán in hand. He wore a black leather waistcoat, black beard and black glasses. He moved the carrots off to one side to warm the bodhrán. He was leaning back and squinting to avoid the smoke, breathing through the corner of his mouth and blowing the smoke away from his eyes with forced-air from flared nostrils. Holding the bodhrán upside down he rubbed the goatskin in circular motion while warming it over the flame. The frustrated Labrador barked up at the fly. Spews of steam lifted and dropped the lid off the potatoes. Steam was condensing on the window. The bar was jammed.

In the bar the musicians sat under the window with a table covered with full and empty glasses in front of them and banged out the *Mason's Apron*. Ashtrays overflowed and a fog of smoke clung to the ceiling. The two brothers and the Protestant stood with elbows on the high counter at one end – their usual spot. The brother with the waistcoat and the hat had left in rhubarb during the week. An old man with black-rimmed glasses and a black coat sat on a high stool with his back to the wall drinking whiskey at the other end – his usual spot. He left mass early to be the first in. In between, heads and hands clamoured for stout and chatted and shouted over the music. John Mulvey stood pressed with his back to the door gripping his pint tight to his chest. The Circus man was itching to sing and the Tinker with the cravat and the polio limp waited for his turn to play the tin whistle.

Behind the bar pounds were taken, the till rang and change was returned. Glasses were ploshed and washed in cold water on the spot and reused. Pints were lined up in a row, ready for the heads to be put on them, and steam rose from the boiling kettle for the awkward bastard at the hatch that wanted a hot whiskey.

- It's the middle of June.
- It's for herself; she's not a hundert.
- That aul' summer cauld is hard shook.
- Jaysus wept.

Empty glasses clinked as they were collected by handfuls and full bottles sighed as their caps were prised off. The optics gurgled and a blue beer cooler beneath the counter on a beer crate in a tangle of pipes hummed to the demand. An old laundry basket filled steadily with empty bottles that clinked as they were dropped in on top of each other. The old man goaded his son-in-law with round cheeks to sing and the son-in-law started to sing a love song.

As we gather in the chapel here in old Kilmainham Gaol,
I think about these past few weeks, oh will they say we've failed.

People jostled and stretched and turned to see the singer and those who didn't or were too short waited patiently listening. And the volume of the chatter dropped and there was the sound of someone slowly gulping their first fresh mouthfuls.

From our schooldays they have told us we must yearn for liberty,
Yet all I want in this dark place is to have you here with me.

Someone gave out a scolding shush! to kill the final mumbles of intense conversation of the cheek-to-cheek brothers discussing the merits of a mare they wanted to buy. They both chuckled the same way and went beefy red behind their pints. The glass washing and till ringing stopped and pints were supped quietly or not supped at all.

Oh Grace just hold me in your arms and let this moment linger,
They'll take me out at dawn and I will die.
With all my love I place this wedding ring upon your finger,
There won't be time to share our love for we must say goodbye.

John Mulvey straightened himself, lowered his pint, closed his eyes, put out his chest and his neck tingled as the singer's voice lowered.

Now I know it's hard for you my love to ever understand,
The love I bear for these brave men, my love for this dear land.

Others blew slowly upward long draughts of smoke and vacantly watched as it swirled and began to fray. Some looked studiously downward or took extra long to crush under sole a cigarette butt. And some just picked an imaginary spot on the ceiling and stood savouring every word.

And in the stillness, the bar woman sneaked away to prod the roast, the marrowfat peas, the potatoes and the carrots. The bodhrán player never put the carrots back and they were only half done. That bollox and his effin bodhrán. The love song wafted into the kitchen:

But when Pádhraic called me to his side down in the GPO,
I had to leave my own sick bed, to him I had to go.

She continued prodding the roast with a big timber-handled fork and the smell escaped from the oven as the big useless lug of a Labrador salivated at her shoulder. In the bar, in the silence of the song, the stout suppers could get the smell of lamb being roasted. Then there was a loud cheer and a clap as the man with the round cheeks closed his eyes, jerked his head to beat time and finish with all he could muster.

-There won't be time--to share our love--forwe-mustsay--goodbye.

He then reached for his pint and his father-in-law wiped under his glasses and blew his nose loudly with a loose handkerchief that he had pulled by one corner from his topcoat pocket.

The brother with the hat went to bless himself and the musicians under the window burst forth once more, to whoops and cheers and another applause, and the till rang and pints were gulped.

Then, Guard Ryan, in full uniform, appeared in the door glaring at the musicians to stop, but they cut straight into another faster tune and a loud cheer went up.

- That's the gangly fucker, that fella.
- Aye, look at the head on him.
- And an eye on him like a goat atin' cabbage.

Ryan stood in the doorway until everyone drank up and left.

To: Cara Andréa Urzi

Adresse: 13/14 Macleay Street
           Potts Point, New South Wales,
           Australia 2011

Cara Andréa,

I am abroad thinking of my home town of Sydney, to see you again at Bar Milazzo and to take a macchiato together made by that other expat *paysano* Claudio. I miss you my dear Italian friend. I miss you like I miss my city made up of all my old haunts, my family, my dear friends, and all those much loved and renowned of Sydney's inner city street urchins.

The day before departing I came across a man that I have seen about town from time to time for many years. He calls himself Harry Morgan; however, I have never been quite certain if this is his real name as he may have appropriated it from the longest serving WWII veteran of the same name. He roams the inner city much like the man on his maroon moped on high speed, on all the footpaths, who blasts Elvis songs from speakers secured firmly to the back for everyone's pleasure.

I met Harry all those years ago on the corner of Oxford and Brisbane Streets when Surry Hills had not yet been completely annihilated and unravelled by gentrifiers. The White Horse Hotel lay as a vacant shell, rumours of Mafioso biker gangs letting it decay and lay to waste away – I believe they call it demolition by neglect. It was still adorned and crowning with the original crumbling statue, horse-hooves proud in the air – wild and unbridled – the building boarded up.

Harry is known to most shop keepers around Oxford Street and the art school students that tramp up and down that street, too impoverished to catch the bus to the train station. He is a darling of the inner city, one of Sydney's much loved sons. I believe it is because Harry is tuned into life in such a way he doesn't miss a moment of it.

By day he wanders the inner city perhaps unknowingly in search of *derive* – an unconscious-altruistic – *flâneur-par-hasard* – by chance. To me Harry is a reassuring face in the endless hoards of insincere faceless crowds that march in one direction or the other. What is his story? I have often wondered what was the sudden change or the moment of impact that let voices speak aloud inside his mind. He has his ways I am sure, his idiosyncrasies-a-plenty, less able to disguise them as the rest of us who attempt to present ourselves as normal-well-adjusted-beings. A friend of mine told me once that the world is just one big open asylum. He looks better these days, less distressed than those days of my younger self walking up and down Oxford Street, on my way to-ing and fro-ing from art school, saving the bus fare to buy a cup of coffee. He seems more self-assured these days, as we all get with age.

I always took a deep breath when exiting at Town Hall Station. The cool air above ground always a stark contrast to the stale-stuffy-putrid-bowels–below–hot-with-human-humidity. I felt then and now still how the train would deliver me into the mouth of the monster of the world, for me to go into battle with the city. Then making my way to or from art school, I would usually catch Harry standing on Oxford Street wearing his fatigues. He was clean-shaven then, but he had the wild look of disturbed thoughts that marched through his head. As if he had this tinder box inside him; the fuse already lit. So he would carry on and rant, lost in his schizophrenic scatting, angry at the world. I felt the same, raging against it, forever dancing on the edge of the razor blade yet trying to find my place in it.

When thinking of all the words uttered by a person, only a few remain unforgettable to any listener, for these can charm, terrify, humiliate, annoy or haunt even a decade later. There is one word uttered by Harry in the year 2001, all those years ago, that I still recall to this day. I must have had the bus fare that day as I saw Harry from the bus on the corner of Oxford and Pelican Streets. He was in his full army regalia with his matching metal army helmet, waving the front page of the newspaper, overwhelmingly distressed and distraught. Harry was screaming the word on the front page which he was brandishing: it read 'WAR!'

I felt Harry's distress and he was right all along. Why nobody else was screaming along with him I do not know. I wanted to wrap my arms around Harry and tell him the dismal truth. That it would be alright, that our city, a far-flung outpost, would be left untouched, and the world's indifference would let life continue as normal in that city of ours. Wilful ignorance

I then think to a bicycle courier, one of the many that race about town and gather at Martin Place and drink directly from their brown-bottled longnecks on Friday afternoons, on the steps to the GPO Building. However, this one bicycle courier is special to me and possibly many silent others I suspect who traipse the State Street line. In between errands he plays his trumpet for the people of his city, his siren song to the city of the South. Yet his presence and his playing are only for the uptown-Hunter-State-Street-elite where he rides. His sounds catch me and the music resonating, hanging in the air, hold me, opening up my unknowing heart.

When he plays he speaks to all the tears that have filled up my paper heart – he echoes all the great sadnesses I have felt in my life in that city. He plays it all out on the streets of Market, King, Hunter and Elizabeth, killing me, exposing me, undressing me with his playing. He plays out all the darkest secrets of my woodwork heart and my metallic soul which cannot help but trip up on that trumpet of his, echoing all the solemn cries of the past, as I listen intently before having to break away. As I always do, I toss a coin, offer a polite smile and walk on, letting him and his song fade into the crowd, fade into the background, fade into the past, his songbook still ringing out to all the people of the southern skies.

On that last day before departure, seeing Harry on the steps of the Energy Australia Building, on the corner of Bathurst and George Streets, I shared my umbrella with him as it was raining. He told me that he lived in a house now, by himself in Redfern, and he was happy with that. He explained to me that he did not have any money until pay day. I gave him all of my coins – they mean nothing much to me but yet another cup of coffee. In return he gave me a kiss on the cheek, his razor-sharp stubble prickling the side of my face as he moved his face away. As we stood under my umbrella I noticed that he was dressed warmly and he started smoking a cigarette; I smoked one with him.

I always thought of Harry as Sydney's *enfant terrible* and me some sort of tortured *ingénue*. He is as much a part of the city in the way we all are, swallowed whole into the mouth of the monster, making the machine turn as we all do, and he is unable to escape its embrace.

Now I find myself here displaced, lost amongst the buildings in search of my own *dérive*; I am here in Paris to be exact and like that last day in Sydney there is the same sadness that surrounds me yet compounded by the crisis here. It is evident all around this city. I am staying haphazardly apart, yet removed in *la belle quartier* but I know there is always a homeless person somewhere just out of sight. The empty shop fronts becoming the bedroom, the living room, the bathroom of the destitute, giving a vision of Paris Victor Hugo would recognise.

What to make of a world gone mad in this grand open asylum. Or stand roadside on an inner city street corner – screaming – calling out – imploring for others to take note!

And so I am writing from here, to be by your side and to see you once again Andréa, from your friend thinking of all of you back home,

Fayroze.

We played the do-or-dare game, my brother and me. He was a bully and hit me when we were alone.

'I love you, little brother,' he would say as he kneed me in the thigh or punched me in the stomach – somewhere it wouldn't show. 'I'm doing this for your own good to toughen you up. When you're older you'll thank me for these lessons in tough love.'

He was bigger than me so I had to endure. I was never able to return his love.

'If you ever tell, you'll die,' he told me and I believed him.

There was that look in his eye like when the time mum gave him the money to take our pet cat to the vet's to have it put down. He made me carry the basket. We didn't go to the veterinary clinic – we went down to the river instead.

I looked in the basket at the cat. A lot of fur had fallen out and the skin was raw and weeping. I felt sorry for the pathetic creature.

'When are we going to the vet's?' I asked.

Jim had taken the money that was to pay the vet out of his pocket and was counting. He picked out a pound and handed it to me.

'Here's your share.'

I stared in puzzlement at the solitary coin nestling in my palm. Jim never shared anything. Mostly he took stuff or ruined it but he never split. I looked into the river flowing placidly by and was afraid to ask.

Jim removed the cover from the basket and reached inside. He gripped the loose skin on the back of the cat's neck and, lifting it out, held the squirming animal suspended in the air. He was smiling at me as he leaned forward and before I could react he plunged the helpless animal into the river and forced his hand deep, completely submerging the mewling cat. The water boiled as the poor animal thrashed wildly.

My heart was beating crazily as I watched and waited for my

brother to bring the cat to the surface again. The struggles went on for what seemed a very long time. A stream of bubbles rose to the surface. I could see the muscles on Jim's arms straining to keep the animal under the water. When at last he pulled the bedraggled animal from the river it dangled limp and lifeless, water streaming from its emaciated body. I knew then why my brother had given me the pound. By accepting the money I was an accessory to the crime.

To get back to the do-or-dare games he made me play.

I had to run across the railway line just before the train hurtled past. I had no option. Jim would propel me on to the track and I had to scamper to safety on the other side. Once a train clipped my heel. I limped for weeks afterwards.

He would throw me in the river, even though I couldn't swim, with the task of getting to the far bank. I would plunge into the water and sink and like that poor cat flail the water madly, arriving half-drowned at the opposite bank. With Jim screaming at me to get back immediately I had to undergo the whole terrifying process in reverse. When I crawled exhausted back onto the river bank my brother would kick and punch me and accuse me of being too slow.

'A man with no arms could have done better than that,' he would scoff.

I survived these and many other such ordeals. To be fair, Jim would take up the challenge also though he had the advantage of going in his own time.

One day the road menders were in full flow with the massive machines and pungent-smelling mixes that tickled the nose. A huge roller trundled up and down pressing the mix of tarmac and gravel into a flat surface fit for vehicles to speed along. The works were a perfect place for young boys to get dirty and get into mischief. Our dare was to run across the fresh tarmac in front of the giant roller.

Jim held my jumper so I could not go too soon. I thought he was leaving it too late when he punched me in the back and sent me stumbling into the path of the roller. Perhaps my brother was right and these tests built into me a survival mechanism, for in spite of the dangers he subjected me to I am here to tell you my story.

I got across the tacky tarmac with millimetres to spare.

I stood behind Jim as he prepared to carry out the same dare. I glanced down at his feet and saw his lace had become undone. Carefully I crouched down and tied them for him. At the last moment Jim launched himself across the fresh tarmac. His feet tangled and he fell headlong.

I watched with interest the roller grind on, flattening all before it. There was not a bump or hesitation as it took his hand and then his arm. His mouth was open and I suppose he must have been screaming but I couldn't hear him above the roar of the machinery but then the roller took his head and it didn't matter anymore.

After that there was a lot of confusion. Workmen ran up to stare at the peculiarly dyed roadway. Some of the colours reminded me of the clothes Jim had been wearing. There were dark reds too and some flesh colouring. It didn't look anything like my brother.

There wasn't much shouting. The roller driver was being sick in the gutter. He must have had carrots for his dinner for I noticed pieces floating in the slurry.

The foreman was talking into a phone. Some of the onlookers had phones too and they were taking photos. I noticed the roller had missed Jim's trainers. I could see the laces where I had tied them together.

MATTY   AOIBHEANN MCCANN

I have resisted being followed all my life. I'm the middle child of a large Irish family. The eldest three didn't want to be followed, so when the youngest three tried to follow me I shrugged them off with learned threats or expressions of boredom. Now here I am trying desperately to be followed by making witty concise remarks. In person I am funny, in the pub especially, but this doesn't seem to translate to Twitter. It makes me jittery but I am looking around for a job these days, as the writing isn't paying off and apparently tweeting is the must-have skill. It used to be Microsoft Word, now it's Twitter.

I am not a liker and sharer of cute internet animals. I am not fuelling the desperate trade in cuteness. Inane kittens that twirl around helplessly on top of once-precious vinyl on turntables, which are probably dispatched to cat rescue as soon as they stop. So I see this Twitter link, 'Cutest baby sloth in the world'. I decide to retweet it in a bid to get more followers.

Cute is a word that despite my resistance seems to seep through my veins from time to time eliciting a helpless kind of emotion within. When I was growing up 'cute' meant a very different thing. If you were cute it meant you were essentially untrustworthy, albeit in an admirable way. If you were cute, you had somehow got one over on someone somewhere who probably deserved it. There was no time in those days to be thinking things were cute in the way we do now. Not with a load of kids to raise on Haughey's tax regime, with kittens to drown and lambs to slaughter. It made sense; if you started feeling things were cute in the 'awh' way, where would you be? Starving on Easter Sunday, over-run by cats and trampled on by out-of-control kids who'd turned on you because you let them away with murder. All because you'd mistaken the meaning of the word cute.

There he is on the link, big eyes, ringed in black, slow moving and innocent. His paw passing an American woman a flower.

'AWH, Mr Matty', she says, 'thank you.'

It is unclear whether he means to pass her the flower or whether it has just stuck to his claws and he is just signalling for it to be removed pronto. I watch it again. Then I take the fatal step down the road of doom. I show the video to my teenage daughter.

My daughter was raised far from where I was in every way. Only child, city born and bred, no chores, no elder sisters to fend off or younger brothers to shrug off. I love her but she is part of the facebook generation. I understand little about her life. She is the teenager they talk about on the radio in outraged tones. Riddled with playstation and porn, refusing to go outside and play, fed on frozen pizza and takeaways. Never slapped, rarely shouted at, destined for a useless college course like Media Studies if she fails her audition for *X Factor*. The radio show hosts sigh as we hear outraged tales of a generation destined to never-ending doom, eating disorders and, worse still, unrealistic sexual expectations.

When she sees Matty she is like a thing possessed.

'MUUUM,' she wails. 'We have to have one. I love him.'

It is unusual for her to be so enthusiastic about anything these days, especially anything I introduce into her life. So I encourage it for a while then promptly forget when it is time for Coronation Street. Just when it reaches its thrice-weekly cliffhanger ending, she rushes downstairs and bursts into the room.

'Mum, Mum, guess what? We can have him! I emailed the sanctuary and they are looking for a home for him. No waiting, no expensive food, he eats flowers, they said he'll sleep most of the time! Please say yes!'

I look at her excited face, which I haven't seen the like of since primary school, and what choice do I have but to agree?

'OK,' I sigh. 'That sounds fine in theory but what about cages and bedding? Vaccinations and licences, I mean...'

'All covered,' she interrupts.

'... but how will we get him here?' I say, trying to delay the inevitable.

'Don't worry about that, all sorted. He'll be here tomorrow.'

She leaves the room and thumps quickly back up the stairs, probably in a bid to update her facebook status.

'Isn't there a home visit or something?' I call up after her but there is no answer.

The courier has to ring three times before I shuffle to the door in my black fleece dressing gown. I don't ever remember being woken this early on a Saturday since she was a toddler. I hastily scribble my signature or what passes for it with a plastic pen thing on a handheld screen. Behind him is a large wooden box with holes in the top. He leaves rather quickly.

She appears behind me, looks over my shoulder then pushes past with a gasp and tries to peer into the holes.

'Mum, Mum, I can see him. Help me open the box.'

Not wanting to discourage her from getting up early on a Saturday morning and actually getting some fresh air, I am nevertheless conscious of blinds twitching across the road. I am only in my dressing gown, which has seen better days. I wrap it around me suddenly in case a freak gust of wind reveals all. Then I look at her in her short pyjamas and yank her in by the vest top.

'Get dressed first,' I hiss.

That's when we hear the voice from within.

'Just use a crow bar on the top, for God's sake,' says a growly American voice.

I am dumbfounded, my daughter seems to take it in her stride. Clapping her hands and jumping up and down, grinning, probably writing her status update in her mind. Anything is possible for the internet generation, maybe this is something the radio talk shows have missed. Maybe there is hope for her after all. All thoughts of flapping dressing gowns go out of my mind along with the 15 year old in short pyjamas, though we're probably being filmed on someone's phone at this stage. I turn and go out the back door and into the shed for a crowbar.

When we prise off the lid, there he is looking up, still from within a cage so I reach to unfasten the clip. He beats me to it. He undoes it and starts climbing out. We stand back amazed. He isn't smiling or doing whatever had passed for a smile on Twitter where we saw him last. In fact he looks distinctly angry as he lopes past us into the house and leaves us struggling with the crate. The neighbours have gone beyond curtain twitching and have come out of their houses to stare. I pull my dressing gown to me and yank my daughter in by the shorts for the second time that day, slamming the door behind us.

He is already in the armchair, there are yellow rose petals around his mouth, the remains of the roses I got for Mother's Day. Ostensibly from my daughter but clearly purchased by her father. Guilt roses but his young girlfriend probably disapproves. Headless now, the stems jut out from the milk jug on the mantel piece. My daughter is delighted and runs to pick him up; he resists by stiffening and rolling his eyes.

'Not now,' he says, wearily. 'Have you heard from Jason?'

'Who?' I say. Still incredulous I am talking to a sloth.

'My agent,' he says impatiently.

'Oh,' I say. 'Is he a wildlife agent? I knew there'd have to be a home visit or a permit or something.'

'No,' he rolls his eyes again. 'You know, an agent agent. I found a guy who is going to capitalise on the whole Youtube thing. 300,000 hits in the first week. It's gone viral. Should get me out of this dump pretty fast, t-shirt deals, sponsorship, advertising, you know.'

My daughter is speechless with delight despite his obvious rebuff. I am not sure what to say, so I go and make a strong coffee.

He asks for a bath later. I offer to put on the hot water but he grimaces.

'Have you not watched the other videos?' he asks aghast.

So we do. They feature him and his fellow orphaned sloths being bathed in organic green tea leaves and put up to drip dry by the claws after. He looks cute again in the video hanging upside down so I decide to try it.

I fill the bath and add the contents of several bags of green tea that were not, as he points out, organic.

It is a disaster; the ground-up tea stuck to his fur and when I try to help him up to dry on the clothes horse it collapses under his weight. He ends up lying on the sofa watching *Big Brother* with my daughter. He leaves a huge stain with ground-in tea but he likes *Big Brother*. He says he thought his agent might get him on it. 'Jason' still hasn't called.

Days turn into weeks. Sometimes he disappears when I am upstairs writing. Asking him where he goes yields no results. I ask my daughter, she says he tells her that he is seeing his agent. We begin to whisper about him out of earshot, avoiding the sitting room where he watches endless reality TV.

'He says he was at the cinema today signing t-shirts with his agent,' she says or something equally ridiculous. I roll my eyes and she suppresses a giggle.

'Classic Matty,' she says.

I wonder what he is really doing during the day. I reckon he is visiting the neighbours asking to be let in and regaling them with tales of his fantastical Youtube fame existence.

He comes out once to tell me off for calling my daughter 'Baby Brat'. I have done so for years and she has somehow let me away with it. He has patented the phrase he says, for t-shirts. I am aghast.

'But you can't,' I say, 'that's my nickname for her.'

'Trademarked now,' he says. 'I could charge you for using it.'

I never see the t-shirts though he says they are for sale online with a picture of him, emblazoned with the words 'Matty the Baby Brat' on fair trade cotton.

They come for him one day in a truck with a cage on the back.

'Ah, Jason must have sent them,' he says, relieved. I think it must be the neighbours who sent them, they have finally complained about a wild animal living in the suburbs.

We wave him goodbye and the neighbours come out to stare.

He waves regally from the back of the truck through the mesh. My daughter is filming it on her phone.

'Classic Matty,' she laughs as she runs upstairs to upload the footage to Youtube.

I go in to tidy up. The phone rings, it is Jason. He asks me am I interested in writing a book, *Baby Brat. My Life with Matty*.

I knew Twitter would pay off.

TWO EYES WATCHING   MARY MCGILL

I was at a training day for work once with this awful annoying 'facilitator'. He had a head on him like a boiled ham wearing glasses and a big tawny moustache that belonged in a joke shop. God, he was insufferable.

'Tell us something you *know*, Beth,' he said during one of those group sessions where everyone has to volunteer some utterly useless bit of trivia about themselves. 'Tell us a little bit of your personal wisdom.'

I said, 'what you know and what I know are two completely different things, even if they look to be the same thing on the surface.'

Well, he gawked at me as if I was after coughing up kittens. I suppose I could've elaborated but how could I expect a man like that to understand, to *know* why, for example, I spent so much time hiding beneath the kitchen table when I was nine? Or why whenever my husband looks at me a certain way I feel like heading for Timbuktu?

I'll say this for the kitchen table: it was a calm spot, if not a comfortable one. There's only so long a bum can handle a tiled floor for, no matter what age you might be. I'd sit there, or lie there if I was feeling particularly slovenly, watching through the chair legs my Mam's slippered feet moving about from cooker to sink as country music twanged on the radio.

In my head I can be beneath that table anytime I want. Close my eyes and I'm back there, breathing in the juicy air, thick with the smell of roasting beef. Down the hall my father roars something at the television as a crowd cheers in a euphoric burst.

My eye is drawn to a speckle of glass, glinting by one of the chair legs like sunlight on water. It makes me think of snow, thick as a duvet. We're walking through a hushed, white countryside, down to a crystalline lake, where I dipped my red wool glove in, feeling the ice-water burn my fingers until Mam whispered, 'stop it, Beth! Stop it before your Daddy sees you!' But Daddy can't see me, I thought; Daddy is just a black dot way over on the hill. He can't see me. Not unless he has super powers – and he doesn't.

The broken glass comes from a jug Mam dropped when Daddy surprised her, surprised her with a slap that sounded like a cap gun shot right into her face.

Afterwards she peered beneath the tablecloth.

'Daddy is tired,' she said, pulling me to her chest. 'You were a good girl, Beth. He didn't know you were in there. You mustn't tell him. Promise me now? Promise me you'll never tell?'

Her heart made a booming noise in my ear. One of her tears fell on my eyelid, a warm raindrop. She brushed it away. When I looked up, she was smiling, trying to pretend the red swell in her cheek wasn't really there.

'Daddy can't help it,' she said, smoothing my hair. 'He gets upset.'

She gave a little shrug, brushing a feathery hand over the pinprick of dried blood on the hem of her apron. She asked in a bright voice if I was hungry and would I like some cake.

I wanted to be sick. I wanted to power hose the sickly-sweet smell of whiskey off myself and everything in the house. I wanted to burst my father's red balloon face with a sharp pin, watching in satisfaction as the air wheezed out of him while he floated away, up into a clear blue sky.

The sound of a key in the front door makes me jolt. I pull my knees under my chin, dry my eyes against the rough denim of my jeans. Someone calls my name, stepping onto the bare kitchen floorboards, disturbing dust motes. They rise like dandelion seeds on a summer breeze.

Why can't I stop coming home? It's a shell now, stripped and emptied; its past is a fading watermark visible only to me.

'Beth?' my husband says, his shoes scratching this way and that as he looks around. 'Beth, where are you? We're not supposed be here with the sale going through. You know that.'

Know? I feel like screaming, like lifting this table over my head and throwing it at him. Do you really want to hear what I *know*?

In my mind I see my mother, leaning over the glowing oven, rose-patterned mitts on her hands as she reaches for the stew dish. I'm telling her about school, peeking out at her with my legs crossed like a little genie. The kitchen is toasty and homey until he arrives, letting the back door swing so wide open the night sweeps in uninvited.

'What's for dinner?' he says, taking off his coat, letting it fall into a damp heap on the tiles. Lying there, it reminds me of a giant black slug.

I'm not hungry anymore. I draw my arms across my tummy, waiting for what I know will happen, what always happens.

'Stew,' my mother replies, the cutlery drawer clanging as she opens it. I can't see all of him, only his boots glistening with wet muck, but it's as if I can smell him, studying her, his face brewing a storm.

Right where my husband's standing, that's where the stew fell with an almighty clatter, splattering across the floor like vomit, burning through my school socks before I had the chance to scream.

Afterwards, rusty blisters the size of pennies covered my legs. My husband asked me once about the scars. I told him I'd pulled a teapot down on myself as a toddler because everyone thinks my father was a gas fella, even him. *A great man in death as he was in life*, the priest said at the funeral. But I don't think that. I never did because I *know*.

POETRY

THE SAFFRON GATHERER   CLARE MCCOTTER

Walking the hour before dawn
to fields gravid
with mauve and deep striated purple
she carries a black bag
oozing honey and thural herbs.
Sky oblation offered
for a crop harvested by hand alone
no tools for cutting
plucking, pulling used.

Humming half-forgotten cords
in numinous autumnal light
she waits for time
to reveal *rosilla* the saffron rose.
Its spindly cinnabar stigma
released from any
supporting stem
with the merest murmur
of un-gloved hay-scented skin.

Crouching in white silky air
she places threads
fought for by perfumers
and Persian physicians
Phoenician traders
and Sumerian magicians
on warm liquescent earth.
Each nascent filament stroked
with a dark horse hair.

As self is subsumed in red-gold
fruit of a crocus womb.

WOMAN ON A COOL CONCRETE PORCH
ELLEN BLACK

I wish I lived in a house with a big front porch.
I long to sit outside
on blue-faded concrete that is always a little cool
even when summer blows inferno
over a mirage of sticky days
and nights, leaving me
wilted and soggy, breathing in the earthy smell of life.

I want to revel in sweet-green grass
freshly cut, looking trim and neat
ready to show off its new hairdo to each
and every rowdy dog and haughty cat that pads by.
I want to sit idly and watch cars saunter past.
I would create a different destination for each driver – sending one man
to a secret bedroom that has been cooled
with lavender and tightly drawn curtains.
I would wave slowly at a woman in wrinkled yellow, knowing
that she's on her way to a popcorn afternoon
where she'll lose herself
in a dark, chilly movie theatre, forgetting
for a few moments
that this is her loneliest season.

I dream of swatting flies away
from a lukewarm glass of lemonade that sits
next to me, knowing I should get up
before my rear end starts to ache
but refusing to move, listening to the shrieks
of kids happy to be out of school
remembering younger-year days when the heat tickled
me with whispers of something exotic
and far away, and I saw a future me – a woman
who was unafraid – who would show up to dinner, wearing only
a black slip and red toenail polish.

SEEING YOU BLEED   MAIRÉAD DONNELLAN

It came from a deeper place,
angrier for that,
a shock of red berries,
glorious mysteries,
scattered.
It fell fast, slid
down porcelain,
spun clockwise back
towards earth.
It left its mark
on a white pillowslip
that would not stanch
your wound
and for a while it lay
under my fingernails,
stayed on the tiles for days,
filling the cracks.

CORROSION   MARIA HIGGINS

All of life is in this moment,
the hitch of their breaths before they kiss for the first time.

I should have realised even then that pretending all of this was about
someone else,
was me protecting my paper heart; the
cracked floorboards of my ribs.

Shivers, shivers; the length of his body.
Rain washes all the colour from the street;
Turns her to liquid in his arms.
'I'm so tired of never seeing the same bed twice.'

People seem different when you learn them through their mouths,
the dark arc of it like night coming across the sky.

No one seems real the moment before nightfall.
It is silver and raining
the hinge on her heart has been rusting for years.

THE SWIMMER   FAYE BOLAND

Standing like a sentry to attention
triangular framed, lean and lithe
you cut a perfect incision,
neat, clean, crisp.

The smooth turquoise sheet sucks you in.
The cool water pulses, swish swoosh
as its meniscus is sliced by sinewy limbs.
You swim with the purpose of a predator,
a dolphin in disguise.

I strive for your elegance. My words flail
on the page. Fingers freeze.
I am a poor imposter.

FEATHER   MARY WALKER

When flight has lost its charm and a feather takes leave of its post
It does not fall
Rather it reminds the air that cannot whistle through its barbs
Of the chill of winter held at bay
Of the heat of summer it stayed
Or of lake's moisture that could not pass
No the feather does not fall
It carelessly romances gravity
Free of a freefall to remind us
Of the respect it commanded
From the air, the water, the land,
And you
Because we all want wings.

CHEETAH   PATRICK DEVANEY

While the others are in sunlight
Beneath the feeding tower
From which a cable
Stretches house-high down the field
And circle round,
Impatient for the daily prize
To come zooming overhead,
He sits alone,
Hemmed-in by trees
That cast a bilious shade.

Watched by admiring humans
The others chase the dangling bait,
The foremost jumping high
To swipe at that swift prize;
He's learned the headless rabbit
Is just food and he'll be fed
Without some silly burst of speed;
Not for him this faux display
For those he'd as soon pursue
As any four-legged prey.

BICYCLE RIDE   PAT MULLAN

I sat on the cold handlebars
my thighs bone-tight to the metal
as you pushed me

Your breath spluttered
hot on my neck
like the engine in
your old Morris Minor

Up and up that brae
you pushed till you seemed
to stand still on the pedals
almost waiting to fall

Hailstones beat down
on my bare legs
till they were scourged red
but I don't remember the pain

I only remember your strength
and your closeness.
We were never like that again.

FREEFALL   KATHRYN DAILY

I unfold like a bolt of white silk
from a cedar chest and a river of waiting
overflows, all possibilities billow out
lighter than air, the helium of hope.

How long will I stay aloft?

Can I make a balloon of white silk,
release from bondage the war-bride
wedding dresses made of parachutes
that could only fall not float?

I will make altars to the wind.

RIVERSIDE   KEVIN GRAHAM

Because you weren't there, because the moment came and went
so quickly I feel I should describe the scene: we were in Galway,
sitting by the river, legs dangling over the seagull-spattered pier,
the sun heavier than usual. A hundred swans were drifting
against the current like it was nothing. I watched their necks
emerge languidly from the shallows, sleeved in the jewellery of
beads of water. A small pool of what looked like mercury settled
in the groove of where the neck joined the back, before the body
erupted in a spree of snowy feathers. They couldn't know
how precarious it was, this thing that trembled like a spirit level,
that held the sun's bright glare, but they carried it with them
without fuss, without complaint – like a soul – their heads
straight as reeds, until they rounded the corner and the reason
I needed to tell you this slipped away with them, out of sight.

PREEMPTION   V.P. LOGGINS

What will it be like when I hear
That you are dead? Will I take
Down and read from your books,
'Digging,' say, or 'Seeing Things?'

Will I look out the window
And think that I see you there
As once you saw your father
Walking wet from the river?

Will the news arrive at night
When the moon is burning
Or in the day when the moon
Is a fading disc of melting ice?

Will I think of you stopping to be
Questioned at a checkpoint, think
Of how you refrained from carrying
Anything more explosive than words

You used to detonate into poems? So
Much of what you made will become
Modified, as Auden wrote of Yeats,
In the guts of the living. Will you

Become your admirers? I swear
That I will feel the sofa shunt
Like your playhouse train. Open
The very ground we stand on.

WHAT SOMERVELL SAW

SARAH O'TOOLE

Everest – June 1924

And slowly they start to seem more far away
Two tiny specks above us climbing strong
We do not know what price we'll have to pay

Mallory decides this will be their day
They check their kit, take oxygen tanks along
And slowly they start to move farther away

It's more treacherous in the snow than on the clay
(A whole chunk of my oesophagus is gone)
We don't know yet what price they'll have to pay

Near the Second Step, a mist veils the display
Of their bravado, they'll be down before too long
But suddenly they start to seem so far away

The mountain's silence chokes us, hopes give way
Two days, we make a cross to tell what's wrong
And, oh, the awful price we've had to pay.

Did they reach the top? Well, who can say?
Poor Ruth, no husband, just a hero's song,
And they never let him die or climb away –
For Immortality – that's the price that you will pay.

THE TALL WAITRESS   ANDREW PIDOUX

I like the tall waitress a lot.
She lumbers around
With all the elegance
Of a giraffe on stilts.

I like how she traverses
The small café tables
With all the smoothness
Of a stretch limousine
At Spaghetti Junction.

I like the way she looks at me
As if I were a tiny village
On some distant plain
Where exotic pygmies
Are rumored to languor,

And I like the way
She likes the way I like her,
That is, in the only way possible,
Taking her all in,
As a drain drinks in a skyscraper.

PINS   KITA SHANTIRIS

Pins secured the butterflies
that my gentle sister chloroformed.
Every swallowtail still reminds me of her.
They were the darkest and most beautiful.

She knew how to name and order
the Superfamily Papilionoidea.
When she was fifteen, she numbed herself
by hiding in a trunk full of mothballs.

Not to die, but to escape.
Sometimes the only way to control
the world is to put pins in a map
and migrate.

Every hinge is made of wings and a pin.
A knuckle pulls them together.
I have her brooch with iridescent wings.
When I wear it, I remember

how I chased her as she ran with the net,
how I pursued her like nectar.
As if I would morph just by touching
the fragile dust of her.

Nowadays, I notice my hands fluttering
like hers when she was talking.
Every swallowtail still reminds me of her.
She was the darkest and most beautiful.

☙ TROLLEYS   JOHN MACKENNA

Is it the constant violence of metal clanged on metal;
is it the everlasting weight of load on load on load;
is it the endless boredom of propaganda on repeat,
seven twelve-hour days in every week,
climaxing in the mad stampede of Friday night and Saturday?

Is it the whining cries of vicious children,
their every whim a scream for some reward;
is it the bump and grind, the stop and go,
the late hours and the early, year on year;
the screeching wheels, the chains at night in rain and snow?

Or is it something else, unspoken and unknown;
some dark metallic secret or some heaviness
that leads to harbour walls and river banks,
sending these supermarket trolleys to their troubled end?

ROSE   ROSS DONLON

For my granddaughter

Codes and letters line the scan
of you at seven weeks, six days.

Darker than a cosmic nightclub,
a semi sweep of light swings

across your mother's womb,
flicks on tucked up head and toes,

a gravity free girl Gulliver
on a nine month space odyssey.

Belly an equator, poles turning
and revolving on your own axis,

you orbit in time, but your lifeline
is firmly attached to the universe.

No wonder you seem to smile
from this one person planet.

In a dark, wild world
pulsing with blood, you're held

cradled in a half circle joined
like hands, like a rose opening.

BOEING 737   CRÉACÓIR Ó'DÚILL

I ndíth ábhair eile léitheoireachta ar naoi míle méadar, léim arís in
athuair
na cartúin ar chúl an taca chloiginn ag an phaisinéir os mo chomhair.
Súim gach brí as na pictiúir bheaga.   Saighead don ghluaiseacht, cinnte
agus is fear óg mé sa tsaol seo a chum Boeing agus Ryanair,
gruaig dhorcha, aghaidh gheal, geansaí glas, bríste gorma.

Tiocfaidh masc na hocsaoine anuas i dtráth
mar anáil Dé, má bhíonn gá leis.   Ní ceart dom bacaint leis an leanbh
go mbíonn m'aghaidh fidil feistithe mar is ceart,
mo scamháin féin ag líonadh.
Cuirfidh mé mo dhá uilleann ar mo ghlúine, mo lámha thart ar mo
cheann,
beidh mé ok.

Is ceart dom déanamh ar an doras is cóngaraí, chun tosaigh nó ar gcúl
nó os cionn na sciathán agus éalú – ar acht nach bhfeicim bladhairí
romham.
Beidh soilse beaga ann le cuidiú liomsa, réalteolaí, más ea nach
bhfeicim puinn,
agus barraíocht toite san chuid den eitleán ina bhfuilim ag lámhacán.
Siúlfaidh mé bealach na bó finne chun na sábháilteachta.

Beidh veist tarrthála orm, thuig mé an rang teagaisc faoina chur umam,
ach ní líonfaidh mé é go mbím taobh amuigh den doras,
ar eagla mo stoptha amhail corc i mbuidéal.
Nuair a shínfear an sleamhnán, léimfidh mé is sleamhnóidh mé agus
rithfidh mé
le mo sheal agus le m'anam.
Nílim baineann, ní chrosálaim mo dhá lámh ar mo ghlúine
ar eagla mo sciorta sleamhnú aníos faoim choim.
Beidh mé slán.

Needing reading at ten thousand metres, I scan
the cartoons on the headrest back in front of me.
I suck all meaning from the little pictures, my childhood
comicstrip -
I, the young hero in this Boeing, Ryanair adventure,
dark hair, bright face, green geansaí, blue trouser clad.

The oxygen mask will descend like the breath of God
in the hour of need. I shouldn't bother with the child
until my own mask is adjusted properly, my lungs fill up.
I'll place my two elbows on my knees, my hands around my
head,
I'll be ok.

I'll make for the nearest door, fore or aft
or over wing, and exit – if no flames bar my path.
A competent astronomer, I'll follow little lights if I see nothing
else
but smoke where I crawl the fuselage.
I'll walk the milky way on all fours to safety.

I'll have a life belt on me, they told me how to put it on,
but I won't blow it up until I'm well outside the door,
for fear I'd stick fast, cork in bottle.

When the slide extends, I will jump and slide and run
for my life and my soul. I'm not a woman, I needn't cross my
hands
on my two knees for fear my skirt might slide up round my
arse.

I'll be saved.

translated from the original Irish by Caitríona Ní Dhúill

THE LOST HEMI-CYCLE OF WOMEN'S WORK
ROSEMARIE ROWLEY

In the pasture land of never-never, your
Broom-tilted scavenging of the archive,
Ready to make all domestic, pure
As the rage you translated live;
Arraignments of taste bedecked your bucolic
Adventures in skin and bone; petals pink
And red spelled romantic reasons, think
Of a heavy army winter overcoat, your frolic
Over the airways, you said, why sample
The dead-ends, the never do wells,
We are a generation of example
Working with doctrine and with magic spells
To sweep up the leavings under our collars
Our last refuge is a redemption for scholars

edito

THE LEATHERMAN   JARLATH FAHY

for Pádraig Stevens on his 66th birthday

When i was young the leatherman came
Regular as clockwork
Every day of the week bar Sunday.
Down the porch
Beret on his head
Bicycle clips above his boots
Shoulders hunched over the handlebars
The spokes purring beneath the mudguard
Stopping at the green door to his workshop
Opening the padlock
And lifting the bike over the lip of the door
The back wheel disappearing into the dark

Then the hammering started
I often sat on the lip of the door
And watched him bent over his bench
In his leather apron
The sleeves rolled up on his collarless shirt
Stuffing horsehair in to horse collars and straddles
with a long claw fork
Tacking hard-wearing plaid cloth to wood
His lips held the pins
The bench bounced everything hopped together
But nothing fell
His feet danced on the sewing machine
His hands blackened thread and string against his apron
The familiar smell of leather

In moments of defeat i sat to watch
The soothing rhythm of his hands and feet
Working with his rolled-up sleeves
The beret on his head
The kindly eyes
Behind his round gold-rimmed glasses
Engrossed in his work.

THE ETERNAL PEACE ACTIVIST   KEVIN HIGGINS

after Donovan and Pete Seeger

When the child soldiers come to our village,
I offer them green, red, yellow
lollipops.

I don't throw grenades at black limousines
carrying Nazi leaders
through Czechoslovakia.

I spend the morning
of the St. Bartholomew's Day
massacre trying to organise
a group hug.

During the Sack of Constantinople
I'm busy writing
a strongly worded statement
against the blood that runs
in the gutters like rain.

Each night I pray
they'll leave it to the United Nations,
Arab League, Warsaw Pact to sort
out amongst themselves.

I ask Genghis Khan
where all the flowers went;
tell Chemical Ali about the universal
soldier who, unlike me, really is to blame.

When you show me room after room
of carefully stacked skulls,
I tell you: the internal affairs
of Democratic Kampuchea
are not my business.

Even if one of those heads
were mine, I wouldn't lift
a fingernail to keep it attached
to its owner, think the peace talks in Paris
should be given another chance.

When a four foot boy clad
in black bomber jacket shoves a lighted rag
through my neighbour's letterbox,
I don't take the easy way out
and familiarize his cranium
with the pavement.

Now, he's six foot eight
and has a gang who go around with him.

NOWHERE PEOPLE   JONATHAN GREENHAUSE

It may have been the rumours of a war or all the bankrupt stores.

Maybe people were tired or sleeping.

Maybe they were dreaming of bustling streets, of sales
 & shops selling out their merchandise.

Maybe they moved to other cities & towns.

Maybe the sun grew too close or maybe too far.

Maybe the tides grew too high & swept them all away.

It may have been an odd hour for crowds,
 a time when everyone's inside,

 a day when people stay in bed & read & talk
 & make love while dreaming of the future's past.

Maybe we were wrong thinking this could last.

It may have been the dirt, or perhaps it was too clean,

but yesterday people were everywhere
 & we didn't think twice nor wonder if.

We didn't imagine what the streets could do without us.

Now the sun shines down on nothing,
 & signs announce sales for no one.

IN A GIFT OF STICKERS   MARY MELVIN GEOGHEGAN

for Joan McBreen

Chagall arrived today –
in a booklet of stickers.
Almost, in the same way years ago
my father pulled out the artist
just as I was about to leave.
Flicking through –
I become his subject.
He invites me to choose a city,
colour, century and time of day.
On reflection, I tell him
'paint me in North County Dublin
in amongst the cowslips
sitting beside my brother
up in Kettle's field on a Sunday.
Our father and sisters down at the water
and our mother resting
on a cloud.'

ROAD WEARY   MICHAEL LAUCHLAN

While he's driving, a dream seeps in,
a girl's face where a lane should be,
an audible breath as a car passes,
a vague elation descending the hill
his tired cylinders are climbing.
He fiddles with the radio, then
shuffles through CDs again.
Etta James can keep him awake
though she's long gone. What pulls
on him seems familiar, a voice
trying to complete a sentence begun
in his childhood, a face composed
of many he has loved. Such thoughts
may kill him, since some aspect
of his being is still moving west
at 75, and thinking about dreaming
lies right next to really dreaming.
At last, Etta says, her vocals
more like sex than song and more
existential than Sartre. He squints
to remind himself that eyes are built
to see large objects like semis, those
orange lights, hung on their underbellies
to offer night drivers a hint
that a cab's headlights and foglights
are really pulling something massive,
more of a rolling warehouse
than a trailing boxkite, but for him,
they suggest the neon behind the glass
of a party store where he hung
as a teen after movies and stole his first

real kisses, stole one, anyway,
from the shocked look in her eyes;
then she taught him how,
and he watched her face change
in that fake light until his legs shook.
From the edge of something
rumble strips call him back
into the drear lines of I-90,
the sequence of hours and miles.

Biographical Details

Ellen Black's poetry has been published in *South Ash Press*, *Illya's Honey*, *The Smoking Poet*, and *Eclectic Flash*. In 2009 she was one of the Pat Conroy *South of Broad* essay contest winners. That same year www.killingthebuddha.com published her first-person narrative, *Heathen Color*.

Faye Boland has been published in *The SHOp* and *Revival*. She has been shortlisted for the Poetry on the Lake XIII International Poetry Competition. She is a member of Clann na Farraige writers' group.

Kathryn Daily was a founding member of Glass Apple Writers and North West Writers. She has been a winner in the Single Poem and Collection categories of the 2001 Charles Macklin Competition, and the 2008 Samhain Smurfit Poetry Competition. Her first collection is *The Comfort of a Wicked Past* (Summer Palace Press 2008). *Fragile Heartbeats of Light*, the first CD of her poetry, was released by Errigal Records in April 2013.

Ron D'Alena was born in San Francisco, earned an MBA at the University of San Francisco, and now lives in Southern Oregon. His work has appeared and is forthcoming in numerous journals and magazines. He is a two-time Glimmer Train Finalist and a two-time nominee for the Pushcart Prize for fiction.

Rhuar Dean is a poet, writer and occasional journalist, based in London, England. His work has appeared both online and in print. More information is available on his website, www.rhuardean.com

Patrick Devaney worked for eleven years in New York, where he was elected to Phi Beta Kappa while studying in City College. He returned to Ireland in 1969 and has since published seven novels, including *Romancing Charlotte*, written under the pen name Colin Scott. He lives in County Cavan.

Ross Donlon is an Australian poet, winner of international poetry competitions and spoken word events. He has read at festivals in Australia, the Wenlock Poetry Festival in England and in Galway and Cork in 2012. Extracts from his latest book, *The Blue Dressing Gown*, have been produced for national radio in Australia. www.rossdonlon.com.

Mairéad Donnellan's poetry has appeared in *Boyne Berries*, *The Moth*, *Windows Anthology*, *Crannóg*, *Revival*, *The Galway Review* and *Skylight 47*. She was recently shortlisted for the Doire Press poetry chapbook competition.

Jarlath Fahy is a former member of the Focus Theatre Group. His first collection *The Man Who Was Haunted by Beautiful Smells* was published by Wordsonthestreet in 2007.

Kevin Graham's poems have appeared more recently in *Antiphon*, *Envoi*, *Iota* and *South*. He was selected for the Poetry Ireland Introductions Series 2012.

Jonathan Greenhause is the winner of *Prism Review*'s 2012-2013 Poetry Prize and finalist for this year's Gearhart Poetry Contest from *The Southeast Review*. He received two Pushcart nominations, is the author of a chapbook, *Sebastian's Relativity* (Anobium Books, 2011), and his poetry has appeared or is forthcoming in *Artful Dodge*, *Hawai'i Pacific Review*, *The Moth*, *Popshot*, *Sugar House Review*, and elsewhere.

Kevin Halleran has an MFA from San Francisco State University where he has also taught. His stories have appeared or are forthcoming in *Flights*, *Avalon Literary Review*, *Quarter After Eight*, *Soundings Review*, *Fiction365*, and *Foliate Oak*. He lives in San Francisco.

Kevin Higgins is co-organiser of Over The Edge literary events in Galway City. He has published three collections of poems: *The Boy With No Face* (2005), *Time Gentlemen, Please* (2008) and *Frightening New Furniture* (2010) all with Salmon Poetry. His work also features in the anthology *Identity Parade – New British and Irish Poets* (Bloodaxe, 2010). *Mentioning The War*, a collection of his essays and reviews, was published by Salmon in April 2012. His fourth collection of poetry, *The Ghost In The Lobby*, will be published in March 2014.

Maria Higgins is an eighteen-year-old student in her second year of college in the National University of Ireland, Galway. She is studying for a Bachelor of Arts with Creative Writing.

Michael Lauchlan's poems have appeared in many publications including *New England Review*, *Virginia Quarterly Review*, *The North American Review*, *Innisfree*, *Thrush*, *Crab Creek*, *The Tower Journal*, *Nimrod*, *The Dark Horse* and *The Cortland Review*, and have been included in *Abandon Automobile*, from WSU Press and in *A Mind Apart*, from Oxford. He has recently been awarded the Consequence Prize in Poetry.

Harriet Leander was born in Helsinki, Finland attended art college in Stockholm, Sweden and now lives in Galway. Her work has been exhibited at the Rory Mitchell Gallery, Oslo, the Town Hall Theatre, Galway, Galleria Dix, Helsinki and the Galway City Museum in the last year.

V.P. Loggins has been published in *The Baltimore Review*, *Memoir (and)*, *Poet Lore* and *The Southern Review*, among others. He is the author of *The Fourth Paradise*, a book of poems about the Irish immigrant experience, and *Heaven Changes*, a Pudding House chapbook. He is author of a critical book on Shakespeare and co-author of another.

Nigel Jarrett is a freelance journalist and music critic, and winner of the Rhys Davies Prize for short fiction. His début story collection, *Funderland*, was published by Parthian in 2011 and was long-listed for the Edge Hill prize. His début poetry collection, *Miners At The Quarry Pool*, is forthcoming from Parthian. He is also the co-editor of *The Day's Portion*, a collection of journalism by Arthur Machen. He reviews poetry for *Acumen* magazine and jazz for *Jazz Journal*. Since 1987 he has been music critic of the *South Wales Argus* daily newspaper. He lives in Monmouthshire.

Aoibheann McCann is a native of County Donegal who has lived in Galway since 1992. She published her first poem in 1995 in *The Edge* and went on to write columns in *Xposed* and *The Galway Independent*. She is working on her first novel.

Deirdre McClay has published stories in *The Irish Times*, *The Sunday Tribune*, *Crannóg*, *Boyne Berries*, *Wordlegs*, *Ranfurly Review*, *The Linnet's Wings* and *Friction Magazine*. She has been a winner in The Lonely Voice Short Story Competition, Highly Commended in Doire Press International Fiction & Poetry Chapbook Competition, and was nominated for the Hennessy First Fiction Award in 2005. She is a member of the Garden Room Writers' group and a regular reader at North West Words.

Philip McCormac is the author of twelve Black Horse Westerns published by Robert Hale, London. *Brother's Blood* is due from Sage Word Publishing and *Hornstone* is forthcoming from Black Horse.

Clare McCotter's haiku, tanka and haibun have been published in many parts of the world. She won the IHS Dóchas Ireland Haiku Award 2010 and 2011. In 2013 she won The British Tanka Award. She has published numerous peer-reviewed articles on Beatrice Grimshaw's travel writing and fiction. Her poetry has appeared in *Abridged, Boyne Berries, Crannóg, Cyphers, Decanto, Iota, Irish Feminist Review, Revival, Reflexion, The Moth Magazine, The SHOp* and *The Stinging Fly. Black Horse Running*, her first collection of haiku, tanka and haibun, was published in 2012.

Mary Róisín McGill regularly reviews books for RTÉ Radio One's *Arena* and is the co-founder and editor of Irish women's website Fanny.ie. In 2013 her fiction appeared in *The Bohemyth* and *Wordlegs*. She was shortlisted for the Penguin/RTÉ *Guide* short story competition and the *Irish Times* Legends of the Fall competition and longlisted for the 2013 Over the Edge award. She blogs at www.wordsbymary.com.

John MacKenna is the author of seventeen books – poetry, fiction and memoir. His current collection *Where Sadness Begins* was published by Salmon Books. His novels *Clare* and *Joseph* will be published in 2014 by New Island Books.

Conor McManus has had his short stories and poems published in *Crannóg, The Stinging Fly, Force 10, The Linnet's Wings, The Leitrim Guardian* and *The Moth*.

Mary Melvin Geoghegan's last collection *Say It Like a Paragraph* was published by Bradshaw Books in 2012. She won the Longford Festival 2013 Poetry award for her poem *The Geography of a Writer*.

Pat Mullan is a thriller writer, poet and artist. He was born in Ireland and has lived in England, Canada and the USA. He now lives in Connemara, in the west of Ireland. You can visit him at: www.patmullan.com.

Clairr O'Connor, poet, playwright, novelist, lives in Dublin. Her fourth collection of poetry, *So Far*, was published by Astrolabe Press in 2012.

Pat O'Connor was a winner in the 2009 Best Start Short Story Competition in *Glimmer Train*. In 2010, he was shortlisted for the Sean O'Faolain Short Story Prize. In 2011, he was shortlisted for the Francis MacManus Award and won the Sean O'Faolain prize. In 2012 he was shortlisted for the Hennessy New Irish Writing Award and the Fish Short Story prize. His radio play, *This Time it's Different*, was broadcast on RTÉ Radio 1. His stories have been published in *Southword, Revival*, the *Irish Independent*, and broadcast on RTÉ Radio 1.

Gréagóir Ó Dúill has taken top prize in the Oireachtas for a collection and at Strokestown for an individual poem in Irish. The poem *Boeing 737* was awarded Duais Cholmcille at Strokestown International Poetry Festival in May 2013 as best poem in Irish or Scots Gaelic. He teaches contemporary poetry at the University of Ulster. Doghouse published his second collection in English, *Outward and Return*, in 2012. His translator and daughter, Caitríona Ní Dhúill, is head of German at Durham University.

Sarah O'Toole works as a theatre practitioner and lecturer. She was the winner of the Aran Islands/Hillstead poetry competition in 1997 and travelled to Connecticut to read at the Sunken Garden Poetry Festival with other emerging poets from both sides of the Atlantic. She has since published in *Emerge Literary Journal* and *The Irish Left Review*. She has also written two plays which have been performed in Ireland.

Andrew Pidoux's collection of poetry is *Year of the Lion* (Salt Publishing, 2010). He won an Eric Gregory Award in 1999 and the Crashaw Prize in 2009. Recent poems of his have appeared in *Envoi*, *New Walk*, *Poetry Review* and *Poetry Wales* and stories in *Litro*, *Staple* and *Stand*.

Rosemarie Rowley's *Flight into Reality* (1989) is the longest original work in terza rima in English and is now available on CD. She has also written in rhyme royal and rhyming couplets. She has four times won the Epic award in the Scottish International Open Poetry Competition. Her books in print are: *The Sea of Affliction* (1987), one of the first works in ecofeminism, and *Hot Cinquefoil Star* (2002). Her most recent book is *In Memory of Her* (2004) which includes *Betrayal into Origin – Dancing & Revolution in the Sixties*, an 80 stanza poem in decima rima, and *The Wake of Wonder*, a regular sonnet sequence, all books published by Rowan Tree Ireland Press, Dublin.

Kita Shantiris (Curry) is a licensed psychologist who has served as CEO of a non-profit mental health organisation in Los Angeles for 14 years. She took 2nd place and had another poem commended in the 2012 Ballymaloe International Poetry Prize Contest and received Honorable Mention in Fish Publishing's 2011 contest. Her poems have been shortlisted for the Bridport Prize (2011, 2012), Anam Cara/writing.ie Poetry Competition (2012) and Fish Publishing contest (2012, 2013). They have been published in *ONTHEBUS*, *Poetry*, *Poetry Northwest*, *Quarterly West*, *The Fish Anthology*, *The Moth*, and *The Faber Book of Movie Verse*.

Stephen Shields has had stories published in *Splinters* and the anthology *Where Freebirds Fly*. His poetry has previously been published in *Crannóg*.

T.N. Treanor has had work published in a number of magazines, most recently *Force 10*. He is a founder member of the Pig Executive, a Manorhamilton-based writers' group. He has also acted with the Crooked Wheel Company's 2012 tour of *Couch*.

Mary T. Walker works full-time as an Assistant Professor of Communication at South Texas College and part-time as a freelance writer. Of India descent she has lived in the USA her whole life. Her writing spans online, print, and academic journals. Check out more of her work at her online portfolio: www.ravalyn.weebly.com

Fiona Whyte was longlisted for Flash 500 Quarterly (2012) and Fish Publishing Flash Fiction contest (2013). She is currently doing a Master's degree in creative writing in UCC.

Stay in touch with Crannóg

@

www.crannogmagazine.com

Lightning Source UK Ltd.
Milton Keynes UK
UKOW05f1540101013

218809UK00002B/15/P